Did she want to? *Yes.*

Dear Reader,

Romance can happen anytime, anywhere. I think that is when it's most memorable, don't you?

You're about to delve into a very special story about a man and a woman whose dreams collide…in a good way! They have to balance their deep attraction to each other while also working for a common goal.

Winning the Doctor is the second book in my Bay Point Confessions series, set in the fictional beach town of Bay Point, California. Be sure to check out the first book, *Winning Her Love*. I appreciate your continued support.

I love to hear from readers. Please visit my website at www.harmonyevans.com to connect with me.

Be blessed,

Harmony

Winning
the
Doctor

Harmony Evans

H HARLEQUIN® KIMANI™ ROMANCE

Recycling programs
for this product may
not exist in your area.

ISBN-13: 978-0-373-86466-9

Winning the Doctor

Printed in U.S.A.

Harmony Evans received the 2013 Romance Slam Jam Emma Award for Debut Author of the Year. Her first book, *Lesson in Romance*, garnered two RT Reviewers' Choice Award nominations in 2012. She currently resides in New York City. Connect with Harmony on Facebook, Twitter or at harmonyevans.com.

Books by Harmony Evans

Harlequin Kimani Romance

Lesson in Romance
Stealing Kisses
Loving Laney
When Morning Comes
Winning Her Love
Winning the Doctor

Visit the Author Profile page at
Harlequin.com for more titles.

Chapter 1

"I'm sorry, but I can't meet with you."

Liza Sinclair bit the edge of her tongue in shock and stared at the attractive doctor hovering in the doorway. He crossed his sizable arms and planted his feet as if he were blocking the entrance to an exclusive club.

If she *had* met him in a club, she would have confided to her friends that he was just the right kind of tall, not overpowering, nor underwhelming. His white, neatly pressed lab coat could not hide his athletic build, but in fact seemed to enhance it in the most distracting way.

Although the tiny cleft in his strong chin lent his face a slice of playfulness, his grim expression was anything but welcoming. His tough-guy stance was a bit off-putting but not insurmountable. Liza inhaled a quiet breath. She wasn't going to allow him to turn her world upside-down at 7 a.m. on a Monday morning.

Who does he think he is?

"But we had an appointment."

Though it was difficult, Liza managed to keep her voice pleasant. She'd come too far to give up now.

A group of nurses walked past her, laughing and carrying on, almost bumping into her in the narrow hallway of Bay Point Community Hospital's General Surgery unit. She twisted her head to the side in mild annoyance, accidentally exposing her scar. It began near her right earlobe and slid to the edge of her jawbone, where it mercifully ended. Though it was narrow, about the width of a piece of yarn and only an inch long, she was self-conscious about it, especially when meeting new people.

Even though she'd worn her long hair down, Liza resisted the urge to place her hand on her neck, having learned over the years that no matter how much she tried, her scar was eventually revealed. She drew in a breath before turning her head back to face Dr. Marbet, and consciously lowered her chin just a bit, hoping he hadn't noticed.

It was too late. Something had changed in his deep brown eyes. Her cheeks suddenly warmed, kindling the thought that his interest in her was more than scientific, more than visceral. But she knew that couldn't possibly be the case.

He thinks I'm a patient.

"You know who I am, don't you?"

His lips melted into a faint smile. "Of course I do,

Ms. Sinclair, but that doesn't change the fact that I've changed my mind."

She stared at the man who had seemed so interested to meet her during their phone conversation a few days earlier. His call had been a complete surprise. When he told her his plans to open a boutique cosmetic surgery clinic and offered her the opportunity to interview, she'd jumped at the chance to design the structure from the ground up.

Though he was only in his early thirties, Dr. Anthony Marbet was a much sought-after cosmetic surgeon in California and throughout the United States. His skills at making beautiful people even more gorgeous were well-known in the entertainment business. His fees were exorbitant. Among his clients were the rich, the famous, people who attempted to break the internet, as well as those who valued their privacy more than a headline.

She hadn't asked how he'd gotten her name. At the time, it didn't matter because she was so excited about the project.

Now, she wondered if the man was playing games. Her stomach clenched as a flurry of negative thoughts raced across her mind. How was it possible that he'd changed his mind as soon as he opened the door and saw her?

She lifted her chin, her inner resolve like steel. "May I ask why?"

His brown eyes locked with hers. "I've decided to go with a professional firm, rather than hire an independent architect."

He can't be serious, Liza thought as she gripped the handle of her leather portfolio case, hoping the action would throw focus on another part of her body, and her pounding heart could slow down.

After extensive research, she'd moved from Denver, Colorado, to Bay Point, California, a little more than two months ago, choosing sun and surf over her beloved snowcapped mountains. Located halfway between San Francisco and the border of Oregon, Bay Point was in the midst of a major revitalization. After years of structural and population decline, people were starting to flock to the little town on the Pacific coast to build new homes and start new businesses.

Making the trek to Bay Point was an opportunity for her to nurture and grow her burgeoning one-woman architectural firm. She hoped the move, though fraught with risk, would pay off professionally and financially.

"But you haven't even given me the chance to show you my work."

She tightened her grip on her portfolio case. There was no way she was leaving the hospital without at least getting the opportunity to share her sketches with Dr. Marbet in person.

He drew in a breath and paused, seeming to consider something for a moment. A few uncomfortable moments passed, and his eyes never left her face. She felt like she would melt under his gaze, but she still held on to her portfolio as tightly as she held on to her dreams.

Finally, his eyes looked at the gold watch that slid from the edge of his pristine lab coat. He stepped aside and swept his hand toward the interior of the room.

"Ms. Sinclair, you have fifteen minutes."

Liza held back a frown and nodded. When they'd spoken on the phone, she hadn't asked how long the appointment was going to be, but she'd assumed it would be longer than it took her to take a shower.

She slipped by him, eager to get inside before he changed his mind again.

She'd chosen a navy silk dress, instead of a suit, to wear to the interview. The classic, sleeveless design made her feel like she was born into money, not someone who'd worked her butt off to acquire it. She resisted the urge to sashay into the room.

Her bare arm whispered against his lab coat as she passed, sending sharp tingles up and down her skin. She could feel his eyes on her back.

Bypassing the leather sofa along one wall, she tried to relax and headed straight for the oval conference table. The half-closed blinds tamped down the morning sunlight and cast a husky glow into the room.

Liza set her portfolio down and turned around just as Dr. Marbet shut his office door.

He ran a hand over his close-shaved black hair. "I'm sorry if I seemed a little rude just now, but I have a heavy surgery schedule today. Still, that's no excuse."

When they'd spoken on the phone, she'd instantly loved his voice, smooth and professional at the surface, pure silk lingering just below. His words weren't exactly an apology, but his tone had changed dramatically and that was good enough for her.

Liza folded her arms, more from habit than annoyance. "I can come back another time if that's more convenient for you."

He raised a brow, as if weighing her offer, and then shook his head. "No. Now is fine. Besides, my schedule is booked for the rest of the week."

Her heart quickened as he approached her and extended his arm. "Let's start over, shall we?"

He wasn't smiling, but his handshake was firm and friendly. She nodded, feeling her shoulders relax just a bit. "I'd love to, and I promise that I won't take much of your time."

He gently let go of her hand, leaving an invisible nest of warmth on her palm.

"Thanks for changing your mind," she added, watching him walk away, his steps purposeful, yet relaxed.

Dr. Marbet closed his laptop, and three flat-screen monitors on the wall directly behind him turned off in tandem. Liza assumed they were used for viewing X-rays and other diagnostic tests.

"I trust you'll make my decision the right one, Ms. Sinclair," he replied as he checked his watch again, instantly re-igniting her nerves.

His athletic frame skirted around the desk and as he leaned against it, he seemed both nonchalant and alert.

"I have my first patient at eight thirty, so let's get started."

He unbuttoned his lab coat, revealing a crisp, blue formal shirt topped off with a bright yellow silk tie that would be outlandish on other men, but on him looked elegant and dignified.

"As I stated on the phone, opening up a private cosmetic surgery practice has long been a dream of mine, so this project is very important to me. Tell me what you remember about my vision for the clinic."

Liza boldly took a few steps toward him. "I recall that you want your patients to feel welcome and at home, so the architectural design will be a cornerstone of the clinic's success."

He shoved his hands into the pockets of his lab coat. "Right. They already know that when they come to my clinic, they are receiving the best medical care that money can buy, so I've got that covered. But I want the building to be designed in such a way that their experience can be uniquely personal."

She nodded in agreement. "Your facility would be the first of its kind in Bay Point. Why do you see a need for it now?"

Dr. Marbet crossed his arms again and stroked his chin thoughtfully. "In this immediate area, the only place for women and men to have a cosmetic surgery or even a non-surgical procedure, something simple like fillers to correct wrinkling, is here at BPC. Even though this is a fine facility, it's still a hospital."

Liza smiled. "Intimidating and impersonal. A hospital isn't the most private place in town." She sighed and chose her next words carefully. "I can appreciate your concern for the locals, but I know that many of your patients are famous."

"Now, where did you hear that?"

She shrugged, not willing to admit that perusing internet gossip sites on a regular basis was one of her favorite guilty pleasures.

"Word around town."

He started to roll his eyes but stopped and grinned. "There are a lot of things you will hear in Bay Point. Some true, some not. But yes, some of my patients are extremely well-known in the media."

"And you want more of them," she prodded.

Dr. Marbet nodded as if the answer were obvious. "Most plastic and cosmetic surgery, that is not the result of certain injuries, is not covered by traditional insurance. Wealthier clients have the funds to pay out-of-pocket for their care. In private practice, I'll have costs, too.

"The lack of privacy here at the hospital is a big problem and keeps many potential clients away," he added.

Liza took a few more steps closer, careful to maintain a respectable distance. She had to know if there was another reason why he was building the clinic, something deeper. Something other than just making more money.

"Are you happy?"

He narrowed his eyes, and she worried that her question may have been too personal for a job interview. Still, she had to know if there was another reason why he was building the clinic.

"You mean here at the hospital?"

She nodded. Even though she was curious to know more about Dr. Marbet than just his opinion on his workplace, it was a good place to start building a connection.

"I've been at Bay Point Community for over six years. The medical benefits, regular hours, a normal schedule, most of the time are definite pluses," he said with a wry smirk. "But there are enough minuses that I feel it's time to strike out on my own," he added, sighing deeply, as if his shoulders were laden with a heavy burden.

Liza clasped her hands together and smiled, happy that they shared something in common.

"I understand. Being my own boss was one reason why I started my own design firm. No one to answer to on a daily basis but my own perfectionist nature."

No one to answer to, no one to blame when she failed and no one to celebrate the successes with either, she noted mildly to herself.

She'd been single and on her own for so long that she'd practically convinced herself she didn't need anyone. All she needed right now was to secure this design gig, and since she didn't know how much time she had left in the interview, it was time to start talking business.

"Dr. Marbet. I can assure you that with me at your side, you'll be able to bring your vision to life."

He gave her a questioning look. "You and your perfectionist nature?"

The teasing lilt in his voice emboldened her, and for the first time, she felt she had his complete attention.

"So what makes you think you're qualified to design *my* clinic other than the fact that, per your website, you've been featured in *Architectural Digest* and *House Beautiful*?"

"Why don't I show you instead?"

Dr. Marbet arched a brow and they walked to the conference table. When they reached it, he stood close enough for her to appreciate that he didn't reek of co-logne, which she hated, or of antiseptic, which she'd expected from a physician.

Instead, he had a nice, clean, soapy smell.

Simple, pleasant and very sexy.

So sexy that it made her want to inhale deeply, but she was the model of restraint, of self-denial. The sit-uation was awkward enough without her acting like she'd never been close to a clean-smelling, handsome man who looked good enough to savor, for one night. Or maybe even a lifetime.

Liza opened up her portfolio case and laid her best work on the table.

"Here are three designs I created, as part of a team of architects, when I was working for a large firm in Denver. One is a private school, one is an office build-ing and the other is a restaurant."

Dr. Marbet's arm brushed against hers, a gesture she was sure was completely innocent, yet her skin pulsed an invisible beat, as he pointed at the first one.

"Ah. Very interesting. I love the open-air feel of the school, and those courtyards scattered about are dif-ferent. Random, and yet organized at the same time."

His eyes danced, and she could tell by the look on his face that he was impressed.

"Yes, I designed those in order to encourage more small groups, rather than the large crowds one would see in a typical school yard."

Liza's heart raced, and even though she knew it would be tough to rein in her growing excitement, she realized she had to remain calm.

"I could see a courtyard area working well for your clinic."

He nodded. "Perhaps as an extension of the waiting room. It would be more peaceful, during what is obviously a very stressful time."

"We could create a separate, private courtyard, specifically for your high-profile clientele."

He braced his palms against the table as he bent to take a closer look at the renderings, and she had the sudden urge to rest her hand against the curve of his back.

"I like that idea, Liza."

She hitched in a quiet breath at the sound of her name on his tongue.

"This design was actually for a client in South Carolina," she continued, as if her world hadn't just stopped. After all, when she got the gig, she'd hear him say her name all the time. Might as well practice subduing her reaction to it, she thought. "They loved it and the climate was obviously perfect for it, but they decided to go for something a little more traditional."

Dr. Marbet looked back and shot her a quirky smile. "You mean boring, right?"

She smiled back, pleased again at his response. It was a good sign. It meant that he was a risk taker, and that, if hired, she would be able to take some artistic chances.

"People pay good money for architects to stretch the boundaries of their own creativity. It's truly a shame when they revert back to traditional design ideas out of fear."

He straightened, and his expression turned serious, turning her momentary joy into concern.

"Aesthetics aside, the surgical units and patient rooms are also extremely important. I plan on having the latest technology, equipment and treatments available at my clinic. The design must be able to support a state-of-the-art facility. Will it?"

"Not to worry, I'm well aware of and have experience in the complexities of health-care facilities planning," Liza assured him, with a wave of her hand. "The innovative care and the excellent patient experience will be the focus of the design, not the other way around."

Dr. Marbet's brown eyes met hers. "We'll need to work together to ensure that the dimensions of each room and unit are appropriate to the equipment it will contain."

There was a sudden, invisible spark between them. Working closely on a regular basis with Dr. Marbet would present its own challenges, namely to her heart. With his good looks, he probably had a lot of women throwing themselves at his feet, and she resolved that she would never be one of them.

She squeezed her thumb and index finger together. "I'm available almost 24/7."

He let out a mock groan. "Aw. No three a.m. blueprint reviews? I'm not on my own yet. You do realize that I still sometimes work odd hours?"

Liza laughed. "If that's what it takes to get the project done, I'll brew a thermos of coffee and adjust my schedule.

"I know we're probably running out of time, so let me show you a few more." She pointed to the second design. "This one was for a technology start-up in Austin.

They loved it, but sadly they lost all their funding the day before we were going to sign the contract."

Dr. Marbet shook his head and whistled through his teeth. "Better before you put pen to paper than if you'd already started."

"Tell me about it. We were very wary of working with start-ups after that fiasco."

He folded his arms. "Don't worry. Money won't be an issue with this project. This is a private clinic, funded by myself and a few key and very wealthy investors." He gestured toward the table. "Tell me about this one."

Liza felt a burst of pride. "This is one of my favorites. The design was for a high-concept restaurant by a famous farm-to-table chef."

He leaned one hip against the table. "What happened to this project?"

"Food poisoning in the chef's other restaurant. A lot of people got very ill, and one almost died. My former firm actually pulled out of that deal first."

Liza shook her head, remembering the stern warnings from their corporate counsel. "We didn't want to be associated with the bad publicity."

Dr. Marbet made a face. "Smart move. I don't blame them."

"Yes, and that experience was so awful that it cemented my dream to break away from corporate and start my own business."

His grin was slow, easy and smoldered all the way to her heart.

Dr. Marbet turned back to the table and examined each rendering again. When he was finished, he turned around. Moments passed. Though his expression didn't reveal anything, she remained inwardly confident.

And this is the part where you tell me I've got the project.

He crossed his arms, his tough-guy stance reappearing, and her confidence began to waver.

"Ms. Sinclair. Although these designs are very good and I appreciate you showing them to me, since none of them have actually been built, it appears that you have no real track record in commercial design."

Though his tone wasn't harsh, Liza felt the snap of his words in her heart. But she wouldn't take things personally—this was too important. She calmly took a big breath, thankful that she'd already prepared for this moment, the not-so-subtle accusation.

"Since I started my own firm a few years ago, my focus has been on residential design. As you've seen in the renderings today, when I worked at Begley, Stuart and Harris in Denver, I assisted on many commercial projects. But as time went on, I quickly realized that both my residential and commercial designs were, and still are, for clients who are more open-minded to an aesthetic that is typically unconventional."

He stared at her, and she felt as though he was testing her in some way.

"It sounds like you and I may have a similar vision," he began, sounding strangely hesitant. "However, you should know, I still have a few more architectural firms who will also be pitching this project over the next several weeks."

Liza's heart sank, and she felt her willpower start to lag.

Competition. Something she loathed and welcomed at the same time. Although she was dying to know the names of the other firms he was considering, she wouldn't dare ask.

"I understand. Thank you for your time," she uttered.

Her voice felt muffled to her ears, as if her throat were lined with cotton. Rejection always hurt, whether personally or professionally, and she didn't think she would ever get used to it.

Liza turned her back on him, put her renderings in her portfolio case and zipped it up. When she turned around, his eyes were curious, leaving her to wonder what he truly thought about her.

Dr. Marbet walked her to the door but stopped short of opening it.

"You know you can try to hide it, but I can tell you're disappointed."

She parted her lips in shock at his words, and at his gentle tone, but he was completely right. There was no use in denying it: she'd wanted to walk out of his office with the project, not empty-handed.

"You can?" she asked, raising a brow. "How can you tell?"

Dr. Marbet chuckled. "I'm not a mind reader, but I can read faces pretty well. When you're disappointed, your lips turn down at the corners just slightly."

She felt her face get hot with embarrassment, and she covered her mouth with her hands. "They do not."

He chuckled a little. "Defend your lips all you want,

but I know you thought you'd be the only one I'm considering for this project."

Though his words hit hard, his voice was light and teasing, causing her to wonder if he was playing with her feelings.

Liza smiled and shrugged, trying to appear nonchalant. "That's because I know I'm the best. I'd like to prove it to you. One can always hope, right?"

"Don't worry." He smiled, opening the door. "I'll be in touch. You're not out of the running yet."

Yet.

That lovely three-letter word left her future hanging by a string, but instead of making her quake with fear, this time she felt empowered because it meant she still had a chance to succeed.

She started to walk out, and then turned around to catch him watching her again.

"I probably shouldn't be asking this, but what made you change your mind about interviewing me in the first place?"

"Let's just say it was a promise I made to an old friend."

Chapter 2

The waves of the Pacific Ocean tumbled onto the sand as Anthony jogged along the Bay Point shoreline just after sunrise. He'd pulled a double shift at the hospital and had been on his feet over twenty-four hours. His muscular thighs screamed for relief through the first mile, easing up only slightly during the second.

The beach was one of his favorite places to run, and lately, to escape.

He took in deep gulps of air as his feet kicked up wefts of sand. Running, no matter what the surface, usually cleared his mind and relieved the constant stress that went with the job of being a physician. His demanding schedule at the hospital meant he didn't have a lot of bandwidth for himself, so he treasured his time alone.

But today he wasn't alone. *She* was in his thoughts.

Liza Sinclair. The attractive architect had impressed him with her confidence, her design portfolio and her never-ending curves. And if he'd had the opportunity to sleep in the hours since he'd met her, he figured she would have invaded his dreams, too.

There wasn't a picture of her on her website, which he thought was a bit odd, and he hadn't been sure what to expect when she arrived for her appointment. So when he opened his office door and saw how beautiful she was, he instinctively knew he was in trouble.

Liza's clear, mocha-hued skin looked fresh and appealing. To his discerning eye, she was a natural beauty. The kind of looks his patients paid thousands of dollars to achieve with expensive fillers and invasive surgery.

He remembered staring into her eyes. The flash of longing there had struck him by surprise. Liza was the kind of woman who could steal his time...and his heart. It was as though his whole life had changed in an instant. He didn't know what the future held other than the fact that he wanted Liza in it.

At least, at that moment.

Deep down, he knew he couldn't afford any distractions. With a twinge of guilt, he recalled his on-the-spot decision to cancel the interview.

Her beautiful face had remained composed, almost serene. Yet the light of excitement had dimmed in her eyes, and he sensed her disappointment.

Even worse, he'd lied to her, telling her he'd decided to work with a professional firm, instead of a private architect, which wasn't true at all.

He stopped running and grasped his knees, gulping in the salty air. He was in great shape and had several marathons under his belt, but for some reason, this morning he felt like he had never run a day in his life.

Anthony yawned as he took his shirt off and slung it over his shoulders. He was due back at the hospital in less than eight hours. It was time to head to his condominium in town for some much-needed sleep—that is, if he could get Liza off his mind.

As he turned on his heel, his phone vibrated against his bicep. Reaching up, he removed it from his armband and slid his thumb across the screen.

"Hello, stranger," he said, good-naturedly.

"What did you think of her?" Doc Z barked. "When I didn't hear from you right away, I got worried."

Dr. Ivan Zander, or Doc Z as he was commonly known, was one of his favorite professors in medical school. After graduation, the two men had stayed in touch throughout Anthony's residency in plastic and reconstructive surgery. Doc Z had even recommended him for a prestigious fellowship at UCLA Medical Center. Over the years, Doc Z had not only become a mentor but also a good friend, and most recently, an investor in his clinic.

Anthony chuckled as he started the long trek back home. "Come on, Doc. You don't fool me. The funny bone doesn't exist, neither does your penchant for worrying."

"That's because everything always goes my way," Doc Z said.

The tone in his voice sounded haughty, but Anthony knew different. Doc had worked hard his entire life but at a mighty price. He was sixty-eight years old, never married, no children. Nothing to keep him warm at night except the soft glow of his computer screen. Instead of investing in relationships, Doc Z invested in stocks, bonds and upstart businesses like Anthony's.

"Stop stalling, okay?" Doc Z continued. "What did you think about Liza?"

"She's perfect." *In more ways than one.*

Like an itch on his back that he couldn't scratch, it made Anthony a little uncomfortable realizing how easily those two words had rolled out of his mouth. He blamed it on lack of sleep and lack of intimacy. Besides, no one was perfect, least of all him.

"Aha! I told you you'd like her," Doc exclaimed triumphantly, interrupting his thoughts.

"Don't gloat, Doc. It's so unlike you," Anthony replied, meaning the exact opposite.

"*Why* shouldn't I?" Doc Z fired back. "She's talented. Smart. And I handed her to you on a silver platter. What more could you want?"

Anthony sidestepped the waves rolling onto the shore. "A little more time to process what this all means would be helpful."

"You think too much. I've done all the work. Now, all you have to do is hire her."

Anthony stopped in his tracks, not caring if his shoes got wet. "Who said anything about hiring, Doc? When you called me a few weeks ago and told me about Liza, I only agreed to interview her as a favor to you. Plus, per your request, I didn't mention that you were the one who had recommended her."

"Which I appreciate, so what's the problem?" Doc interjected.

Anthony huffed out a breath. Liza was the first woman, in a long time, who amounted to more than a ten-second blip on his brain, something that was none of Doc's business.

He started walking again. His sneakers were now wet, and he couldn't wait to get home and out of them.

"For starters, I still don't understand why you asked me. If you want me to hire her so badly, I think I have a right to know."

"I've known Liza's family for years, since she was a little girl. I made her father a promise that I'd always watch out for her. He passed away about a year ago."

"And her mother?"

Doc sighed heavily. "Gone too. Died a year before her husband as a result of complications from botched cosmetic surgery she had done in Costa Rica."

Anthony's heart squeezed in his chest. He couldn't imagine the grief Liza had felt losing her mother and father in such a short time period. Both of his parents were still alive, thankfully, and though they lived thousands of miles away in South Carolina, he was still very close to them.

"That's terrible. I know it's a growing trend to go overseas for all types of surgical procedures. Though the costs can be significantly less than the United States, there are definite risks that many patients don't know about or even consider."

"It's a problem, for sure," Doc replied. "But right

now, all I care about is convincing you that hiring Liza would be a very good thing."

Anthony shook his head. "Now that I know a little bit about her family background, I'm even more uncomfortable with this plan. Is Liza okay? She seemed to be, but I don't know. I need the architect to be on point and fully engaged with this project."

"She's a very strong person," Doc replied without hesitation. "But she needs something different. That's why she moved from Denver to Bay Point. She was successful there but a bit unfocused."

"Yes, her residential work is fantastic, but her commercial work is lacking."

"Minor detail," Doc gruffed.

"Minor detail?" Anthony exclaimed, sloshing through the sand. "This clinic has to be designed right. Why didn't you tell me?"

"I wanted you to meet her and judge her on her own merits. You saw her portfolio. She's great at what she does."

"True. Her commercial renderings were amazing, but none of them has ever been built."

"So? What's the problem?" Doc said. "That wasn't her fault. She told you that, didn't she?"

Anthony nodded. "Yes, but it's still a huge problem for me, and as one of the main investors in this project, I'm surprised you don't feel the same."

"I don't feel the same because I know Liza personally. Trust me, Anthony. She'll do great work."

"If you feel so strongly that she is the right person for

the role, why couldn't I tell her that you'd recommended her? You've put me in a really awkward position."

Doc was silent for moment. "Liza is a very independent woman. If she knew I was trying to help her, she wouldn't be pleased. She can never know that I'm the one who brought her to you."

"Just in case you didn't hear me earlier, I interviewed Liza as a favor, Z," Anthony emphasized again. "I didn't promise that I would hire her."

"You'd be doing me an even greater favor by changing your mind."

Anthony was very curious about Liza. How she would use her creativity, not to mention how she would feel in his arms. However, the situation was making him a little uneasy.

"Let me put it to you this way," Doc continued. "Even though I do have a ton of money invested, ultimately it's your gig and your decision. But I honestly believe that having Liza design the clinic is in your best interest…and mine."

"Because you always get your way, right, Doc?" Anthony said with a smirk.

Doc laughed. "Yeah. Besides, everyone needs a little help, a first chance, a shot at doing something they've never done before. You did, remember?"

Anthony opened his mouth to protest, but no words came out.

Doc was right. When Anthony was in medical school, Doc had promised him that if he worked hard, he would help him succeed. True to his word, Doc had mentored him and opened doors to people and opportunities that Anthony would have never had access to by himself.

He stared out across the open waters. "Going with an independent architect as opposed to a small or even midsized firm is risky. Liza is going to have fewer resources, and since she recently moved to the area, I'm sure she won't have the construction contacts that a full-services firm would."

"She's a smart woman who will navigate her way quickly. She designed my home. You can trust her."

"I don't know, Doc." Anthony shrugged, lifting a fistful of sand and watching the granules slip through to the ground below.

"Tell you what. If you hire her, I'll pay her fee. The entire thing."

Anthony sucked in a breath and whistled "That's very generous of you, Doc, and possibly, very stupid."

"Not at all. I believe in you. I believe in her. Someday, so will you."

"I'll think about it."

"Think quickly."

"So what's on your plate for the rest of the day? Besides making me feel guilty."

Doc chuckled. "No patients today. Just me, a good book and a glass of chardonnay under the umbrella by my beautiful, sparkling pool. And you?"

"Sleeping, and then back to the hospital later this afternoon. I'm thinking about taking a drive out to the construction site tomorrow morning."

"Oh? Take Liza. You won't regret it."

"I'm not so sure about that," Anthony replied, rubbing his temple.

Doc laughed. "Have I ever steered you wrong?"

Anthony ended the call and grimaced, suddenly remembering the sweet, caring tone of Liza's voice when she'd asked him if he was happy.

The question had come out of the blue, and he had to admit, he'd been pondering it ever since.

Happy?

For the most part he was. He had plenty of money, a great career and a small group of close friends. Plus, he was about to embark on a brand-new adventure, building and owning his own business, something he'd dreamed about for years.

He slipped his phone into his pocket and inhaled the salty air into his lungs. The beach was empty at this hour except for seagulls dive-bombing the ocean for their breakfast, and Anthony couldn't have been happier at the lack of human beings in close proximity.

Bay Point was a small town, and everyone seemed to either know him personally or know about him. While it was great for attracting new patients, it was terrible for maintaining privacy.

Not that he'd had much of a personal life lately.

Kneeling down, he scooped up a handful of sand, brought it in for closer inspection. The color was unusual: pale beige flecked with bits of white, green and black. He couldn't have counted the number of grains even if he'd had the desire or the time. But he could count the number of times he'd walked along this beach with a woman.

"Zero," he muttered to himself, as he stood up and angrily pitched the sand back into the Pacific.

Yet, he'd chosen to spend his nights alone.

His demanding schedule had made it nearly impossible to sustain a long-distance relationship with his former girlfriend in Miami, when he'd first moved to Bay Point six years ago. She'd complained that he was more devoted to his career than to her.

Yet even when the relationship was over, he had little interest in pursuing another one, despite the seductive looks he regularly received from local women. That was just asking for trouble in a town like Bay Point, which seemed to thrive on gossip, rumors and innuendos.

Anthony didn't have time to fall in love—with any woman, let alone Liza Sinclair.

Lust, maybe. But love?

He brushed the sand from his shorts, dismissing the thought, and put his shirt back on.

Love was for men with nine-to-five careers, not for men like him. Building his clinic and serving his patients were all that mattered. Falling in love with Liza—or any woman for that matter—was not part of his plan.

Chapter 3

L<small>IZA</small> eased her white pickup onto the gravel and braked in front of an abandoned motel. Judging by the broken windows, chipped plaster and the weed-choked parking lot, the Sunray Inn hadn't had any travelers in years.

She pushed her sunglasses on top of her head and carefully rubbed her eyes, so as to not disturb her mascara.

"Too bad this place isn't still open," she muttered under her breath. "I could use a few more hours of sleep. These morning meetings are killing me."

The doors were covered in signs with faded red lettering warning would-be criminals and the curious that the structure was condemned and that trespassing would be punishable by law. The largest sign of all declared that the place was SOLD. As tired as she was, just seeing that one word energized her at the prospect of seeing the new owner.

Dr. Marbet had occupied her thoughts for the past few days. Some positive, some negative and some deliciously naughty, and yet, all were colored by the cold, hard, truth.

The design project wasn't hers.

Not yet.

Liza scowled and leaned her chin on the steering wheel. Her fingers grazed her scar, reminding her it was there, and that she wasn't perfect.

As if she needed a reminder at all.

She blew out a breath. *Competition be damned.*

Over a sleepless night or two, she had come to the conclusion that she would refuse to dwell on the negative. On the what-ifs. And on the fact that Dr. Marbet was more than just a figment of some 2 a.m. fantasy: he was the key to fulfilling her dreams.

Liza popped in a breath mint to remove the scent of her early-morning coffee, opened the door and stepped out of her vehicle.

"Ow!"

She looked down and saw that the heel of her high wedge sandals had hit a medium-sized rock. Ignoring the urge to kick the blasted thing away, she leaned her hip against her truck and bent at the waist to massage her throbbing ankle.

Moments later, she heard the squashy crunch of tires on gravel fast approaching.

A truck pulled up next to her, swirling a cloud of

dust into her face. It was the same model as hers, but it was black and in better condition.

Straightening, she braced her hip against her vehicle and started to cough.

Dr. Marbet hopped out and circled around his vehicle. "I'm sorry about driving in so fast. I saw you examining your foot, and it looked like you were in trouble."

Her heart warmed at the concern etched on his face, but just as quickly, she realized that was his job. He was a doctor. He was supposed to care.

"No big deal, Dr. Marbet," she choked out, struggling not to cough again. "I'm just going to die from gravel dust inhalation."

"No you won't. I'll take care of you."

His smile seemed genuine and his hand gently patted her on the back, amplifying the butterflies that had begun to swirl inside at his soft touch. It was gentle, yet deliberate, and she chalked that up to his bedside manner automatically kicking in.

As if responding to the perfect antidote, her urge to cough ceased almost immediately. The pleasurable sensations he invoked spread quickly throughout her body.

Moments later, he lifted his hand. "If we are going to be possibly working together, can we kill the formalities?"

She nodded. "I suppose I can manage that, Anthony."

His name sounded so luscious as it tumbled out of her mouth that she momentarily forgot her injury.

"Ouch," she exclaimed loudly as she took a step forward.

He knelt on one knee and visually inspected her ankle. "What happened?"

She grimaced as embarrassment mingled with pleasure at the caring look in his warm, brown eyes.

"I think I might have twisted it getting out of the car."

He balanced his elbow on one knee and kept his gaze on her.

"Clumsy much?" he asked, his tone playful.

"Lots much," she admitted. "I guess I'm overdressed. I probably should have worn flats, but I assumed this location would be paved."

"You look fine," he said, casting his eyes up her body, clad in a soft floral-print dress that hit just above her knees.

Anthony kept his eyes on hers. "May I examine you?"

Despite having grown up in a family of physicians, she never liked going to one. However, she would make an exception for Anthony. This was a chance to be touched by one of the most gorgeous men she'd ever seen.

For medical purposes only, of course.

Her ankle didn't even hurt that much anymore, but she decided to keep that little tidbit to herself.

She nodded her consent and held her breath.

"Tell me if any of this hurts," he instructed, before looking down at her ankle.

Anthony began to palpate her flesh, and she bit her lip as her loins began to quiver with every gentle touch. She could feel the low heat emanating from his palms and wondered what he would do to treat her if she fainted right on the spot.

The pads of his thumbs pressed and circled over her skin, little ripples of wonder that journeyed up through her body. She knew she shouldn't be feeling this way. The man was a physician, and he was only doing his job, but she couldn't help it. His fingers were skilled and felt so good that she didn't want him to stop.

Anthony tilted his head up. "Any pain?"

Liza shook her head. "I think you massaged it all out of me."

He slowly removed his hands from her ankle.

"See if you can rotate it comfortably."

She did as he asked, and though there was a tinge of pain, she'd survive.

"I'm okay now, thanks."

He stood up and dusted a few pieces of gravel from his dark blue slacks. As he did, she watched his muscled arms flex under his light gray T-shirt.

"Great taste," she said.

Anthony looked down at his pants. "What? You mean these?"

"No, not in clothes," she said. "In cars. You have great taste in vehicles."

Puzzlement crossed his face, and she half covered her mouth, realizing that she'd just insulted him.

"Not to say that you don't have good taste in clothes, too," she said, trying to recover. "It's just weird to see you in normal clothes, and not just a lab coat."

He crossed his arms in a way that made her heart skip a beat. His biceps nestled against his sides in that casually sexy way that only some men could achieve.

"What's so strange about it? I'm a regular guy who wears regular clothes," he said, sounding off-put.

"I'm sorry. My dad and uncle were physicians, and I

saw them so much in their hospital scrubs that whenever they didn't have that stuff on, it always surprised me."

He grinned, lowering his voice. "I guess I'm not used to having someone notice."

The man had to be joking, she thought. Who wouldn't notice a body like his?

Their eyes met, and a sudden spark was there. It was indefinable, yet she could feel it and knew he was aware of it, too. She made a show of brushing her hands together as if she could simply rid herself of what she'd just experienced between them.

"There's a first time for everything."

He laughed. "No kidding. I wasn't expecting you to drive a truck."

She put one hand on her hip. Now, who was insulting whom?

"Women can't drive trucks?"

"Hold on. I never said that. But you should be wearing jeans or maybe a cowboy hat. Not a sundress and heels."

Liza stared at him, openmouthed. "I know I'm dressed a bit formally, but I'm here for a meeting, not a hoedown."

He laughed again, and she couldn't help but smile, feeling exasperated and pleased.

"Actually, when I drove up and saw your truck, my first thought was that someone was trying to break in."

She took a quick glance behind her and shivered. "Into this old place? It looks like the Bates Motel. Besides, do I look like a burglar to you?"

Anthony leaned against his own vehicle, an easygoing quality in his stance.

"No. Not at all." He grinned, regarding her. Not in an offensive way but rather curiously. More appreciative of…what? she wondered. *Something.* It was the unknown that made her blush.

She cleared her throat and carefully picked her way over the gravel, being mindful of reinjuring her ankle.

"I'm surprised anybody would know this place is here. It's near the highway but still pretty secluded. I even drove past it a couple of times."

He joined her on the cracked sidewalk that led to the motel's office. "I know. But the sale was listed in a few local papers several weeks ago. Ever since, there have been some issues. A few more broken windows to christen the ones already here."

"The location will certainly give your patients plenty of privacy, that's for sure."

She pointed to the long entranceway. "Those trees lining the private road in here must be sixty feet tall!"

"Yes, I've been advised to get rid of them, but I never will. Privacy aside, those trees are home to hundreds of birds."

"The property is still zoned commercial, I assume?"

He nodded. "Absolutely. I checked with City Hall before I purchased it, and we're good to go there. Of course, once I decide on the final design, we'll have to submit it to the commercial zoning board for approval."

"And there will be construction and other permits to secure as well. Don't worry, I'll take care of everything," she replied confidently, as if she already had the job.

Anthony glanced down at her ankle again. "If you're sure you're okay, I'll give you the grand tour."

"I'm fine. I just need to grab something from my truck."

Liza walked back to her vehicle, ignoring the whisper of pain in her ankle, and retrieved her camera. Taking pictures of the existing property would help her get a sense of scale, although she wished the motel were already torn down. It would have made visualizing another building in its place a lot easier.

"Let's go," she said.

Due to his long legs, Anthony edged out a bit ahead of her. He slipped his hands into his front pockets, stretching the fabric of his pants over his tight buttocks.

"As you can see, the property has been vacant for a while," Anthony explained. "Once you get past the trees, it doesn't look like much from the front. But I bought this place fairly inexpensively, considering that the value is in the land."

Liza caught up to him. "From what I've heard, there's been more and more outside interest in building in Bay Point since Mayor Langston instituted his redevelopment plan."

"Yes, and I was lucky to get the property when I did."

Liza breathed a sigh of relief. "I'm glad to hear that if this project doesn't work out and you decide to go with someone else, the opportunities for commercial architecture and design projects are plentiful. It's one of the reasons I moved to Bay Point."

He pinned his gaze on her. "And the other reasons?"

She paused and turned away to fight back the tears that suddenly sprang to her eyes.

There was no way she was getting into the details of how the grief over losing her mom, and then her dad, had made life in Denver almost unbearable.

Liza turned back abruptly and forced a smile. "Sun, surf and a fresh start, what else?"

Plus the chance to work with a very hot man, she thought. *An unexpected bonus.*

Anthony grinned, seeming to be satisfied with her answer. "Keep that pretty smile on your face because you're about to see something amazing."

She followed him under an arch that connected one side of the motel with the other. Looking overhead, she could see the stucco was cracked in many places, weeds poking through like disembodied roots in some dank underground cave.

When they emerged, she gasped aloud.

"Beautiful, isn't it?"

Ahead of them was a clear view of the Pacific Ocean. Miles and miles of blue, hauntingly still water, framed by the orange glow of the sun rising in a clear sky.

"Amazing," she said, inhaling quietly but deeply. The salty scent of the air was both delicate and mysterious, like a secret that would never be revealed.

Liza tore her attention away from the ocean and focused on Anthony. She had to fight the urge to pick up her digital camera and snap a photo of him.

With his powerful arms outstretched and the sun glowing behind him, he looked like he could be on the

cover of one of those money or entrepreneurial magazines. The guy who'd captured the world and held it in
the palm of his hand. A man who'd made it, and made
it big.

Liza smiled. And it would be she, not some bureau-
cratic architectural firm that moved like a sloth and
charged a king's ransom for its services, that would
push him to even greater heights.

Without warning, a quick fantasy of him in the
same position but completely nude skittered through
her mind. The sun glinting off his black hair, his arms
outstretched, the lower half of him stirring to life right
before her very eyes.

"I'd say the view is priceless," she murmured.

He motioned her forward, and the fantasy ended.
She followed him to the edge of the weed-choked patio.

When she looked down, she almost swooned, not realizing how steep a cliff they were on. All that was between them and certain death was a rickety old wooden
fence. The kind with two long pieces of wood and a
space in the middle, wide enough for a small car to plow
through, like in those old cop shows from the '70s.

Anthony peered down. "Stairs to the beach will be a
requirement of the new design." He pointed to the right.
"There's a narrow opening over there that may work."

They both leaned against the wood, her barely grazing it, him with a bit more pressure, and she felt the
railing wobble.

"Careful," she warned, clasping his arm. Her voice
was sharp, but only because of the flash of fear that had

slid through her body, at the mere thought of something happening to him.

Even though she'd only known him for a very short time, she would be upset that he got hurt in any way, but she wasn't about to reveal her feelings about him. Not only was it unprofessional, but also too embarrassing if he didn't feel the same way.

His eyes met hers, but she didn't let go. "What are you, my guardian angel?"

She pursed her lips and retorted. "If you fall off this cliff, I can't build you a clinic, now can I?"

He moved away from her, forcing her to release her grip, and seemed surprised at her answer.

She took a few snapshots of the motel. When would this man realize that she was just as career driven as he was?

"I wish this broken-down place was demolished. My wheels are already starting to turn."

He smiled, and took another step away from the railing. "Agreed. There are a few loose ends to take care of, and I want to have the architect in place before the demolition. In fact, I want that person to select the construction team for the build."

"That's not a problem. I've already started to make connections and get references from local companies. I think it's best to hire a builder from the area rather than out of town, because they are more familiar with the regulations."

She fingered the lens of her camera. "Once the building is razed, we'll need to have the land graded and surveyed. There are a thousand things to do before we even think about laying the foundation."

Anthony nodded. "I've read up on the LEED rating system. I want my clinic to be LEED-certified, from the ground up."

Liza tilted her head, hugely impressed and excited. Barring his statement about saving the trees to preserve a natural habitat, she never would have pegged Anthony for an environmentalist.

"That's great to hear. LEED certification is the gold standard in healthy, resource-efficient building practices. But going green is going to add to your cost and could extend the project timeline," she warned.

"I don't care about the cost, but I do want to ensure we are using as many environmentally friendly materials as possible."

She smiled. "Building green certainly fits with your vision. It will show your patients and employees that you care about their overall health and well-being as well as every aspect of their experience at the clinic."

"Exactly. My position at Bay Point Community Hospital is secure, and even when the clinic is open, I'll still be a part of the staff but on a part-time, on-call basis. I don't want to rush this. I want to do it right."

Anthony walked over to a small pool. Liza followed and saw that it was empty of water, but littered with trash.

"I can appreciate that sentiment," she said, stepping away from the edge. "I always suggest that my clients use environmentally friendly materials when available. I'm glad you care about the Earth as much as I do."

"Another thing we have in common."

Liza couldn't help noticing how his eyes quickly traveled over her body.

"And another reason why you should work with me, instead of a huge firm," she added, with a grin of pleasure.

They toured the grounds for another half hour. His arm brushed against hers every so often, those brief touches warming her in places the sun never could.

As they walked, she listened closely as Anthony gave her a quick lesson on the flowers and shrubs that were native to the region.

"You're quite the horticulturalist," she said in a teasing voice.

He shrugged. "I don't get to garden much with my schedule. So I'm really looking forward to working with the landscaper. I want to keep as much of the existing plants and vegetation as possible."

Liza took pictures throughout the tour. An hour later, they were back in the parking lot.

"Can I see some of the photos you took?"

Liza nearly gasped aloud. When he wasn't looking, she'd taken some pictures of him. Just for fun, she said to herself, not for fantasies.

"Um. I'll email them to you later today, okay?" she blurted, and stuck out her hand. "Thanks again for the tour. Now that I've seen the land and that incredible coastal view, it will be easier to design something you like and meets your needs."

His fingers stroked lightly against her palm as he

let go of her right hand, making her want to have him shake the other one.

"You're welcome. It was fun."

They both yawned at the same time, then laughed.

A smile stretched across his face. "I gather you're not a morning person?"

"No," she admitted. "But I'm adjusting. I keep my windows open at night, and the smell of the salt water in the air helps me wake up better than any alarm clock."

"As a physician, I'm pretty much on call 24/7, so I have no problem waking up at the crack of dawn, or anytime for that matter."

Liza couldn't help giggling a little bit. "I actually had to tip-toe out of the B and B. Otherwise Maisie would have stopped me to chat. I don't think the woman ever sleeps."

"Or ever stops talking," he laughed. "Maisie Barnell, Bay Point's town matriarch, and the woman who can carry on a conversation longer than—"

"A wave can stay upon the seashore," she finished, with a fake swoon.

His smile deepened, rounding his cheeks. "Very poetic."

Liza palmed her camera and grinned. "Maisie has tons of poetry books in her parlor, so I guess I picked up a few lines."

"She's a great lady, but she's forever trying to hook me up with every single woman in town."

He paused, crinkling his brow. "She means well, but I don't have the heart to tell her that my taste in women is far more sophisticated than what's currently available here."

Liza wasn't surprised Anthony was sought-after. He was rich and handsome, with the kind of boyish good looks that would appeal to most women. However, she disliked when men thought they were "all that," even when they were. The only thing that saved him was the hint of playfulness in his tone.

"Oh, is that why you're still single?" she asked.

"Up until recently, there hasn't been anyone to consider."

Her heart clenched at the thought of Anthony's interest in someone else. She didn't know his "type," other than the fact that it definitely wasn't a small-town girl, and she fought the urge to push him for further details. His personal life was none of her business.

"Don't tell Maisie that she's fired. If you do, she'll redirect her matchmaking skills back to me instead of you," Liza teased.

"Maisie is easy enough to avoid, if you move out of town that is," Anthony said drily.

She laughed. "Not a chance. In fact, I'm staying with her while my house is being built."

Anthony raised a brow, and his grin appeared sympathetic. "You must have the patience of an angel, though I'm glad to hear you're not simply passing through town."

"I'm here for the long haul. I found a great piece of land at a great price. I'm going to build one of my own residential designs. The timing is perfect and I can't wait to break ground."

The smile disappeared from his face. "If I select you for this project, are you sure you're going to have enough time to devote to me?"

Liza widened her eyes. "Devote to you?"

He quickly cleared his throat, and looked uncomfortable. "Sorry. I meant to say my project."

Liza hid a smile and nodded. "I can assure you that I will be completely devoted to the design of the clinic. As far as building my own home, I'm taking my time and Maisie said I'm welcome to stay at the B and B as long as I want."

Anthony heaved a sigh of relief. "I'm glad to hear that. It's really important that whomever I choose can be my complete partner." He gestured back toward the soon-to-be-demolished motel. "In what I'm trying to do here, of course."

He extended his hand again, and she wondered if he'd forgotten that they'd already said goodbye.

"I'm sorry that I got you out of bed so early once again but I appreciate you accommodating my schedule. The next step will be the actual presentation. I'll call you soon with the date."

She kept her eyes on his and boldly trailed her fingers lightly across his smooth palm, before letting go.

As he turned to walk back to his truck, Liza told herself quickly that what she was about to ask was all in the name of continuing to solidify their business relationship and nothing more.

But the truth was, she didn't want to wait days to see him, or hours to feel her heart race again. Whenever she looked into his eyes and felt his skin brush against hers, he inspired long-dormant fantasies that she wanted to flame. If only in her own mind.

"Wait. I'd like to talk more. Can we have dinner sometime?"

She kept her voice soft, yet businesslike, holding back an edge of flirtation.

"My treat. You look like you might need a break."

He turned around, and though he stayed where he was, she could feel the electric pull of his body.

"That bad, huh?"

Her face warmed at his lazy grin. "No, not bad at all. That's not what I meant."

He rubbed his chin with the back of his hand. "I know what you meant. I have been working like crazy lately, and I could use a night off. I do have some free time on Saturday night. Does that work for you?"

"Perfect," she responded, hiding her excitement behind a professional tone. "We can sync up on the details later this week."

If she didn't care about looking like a fool, she would have thrown her keys up in the air with joy. Liza looked back at the aging motel. "There's a lot of potential here. Once this place is torn down, the possibilities are endless."

He dug his keys out of his pocket. "Agreed. The moment I saw the view in the back, I knew this was the perfect place for my clinic."

"If you don't mind, I'd like to come here in the early evening and take some more photos. It will help me as I create the design."

She pointed at the NO TRESPASSING sign. "I don't want to be thrown in jail."

Liza was surprised when he suddenly put his keys on the hood of his truck and walked around to where she stood by hers.

"Sure. You're welcome anytime. However, even though this is a safe area, I would never want you coming out here alone at night."

"Why not?" she asked.

He took a few steps toward her, and his eyes shadowed as they roamed over her face. Then he stepped back and leaned a hip against the side of his truck.

"As I said earlier, there's been some issues with vandals, and I wouldn't want you to get hurt."

Warmth filtered quickly through her body. Though his concern may have been warranted, she could take care of herself.

"I'll be fine, I assure you."

He nodded and waved goodbye, got into his truck and started it.

Liza got into her own vehicle and closed the door, a smile of satisfaction on her face. Their second meeting had gone considerably better than the first. By inviting him to dinner, she would further cement her chances at designing his clinic. In her heart, the job was already hers.

She was so excited she could barely put the key into the ignition. She heard the quick blast of a horn, glanced over and saw Anthony motioning to her.

Curiosity mixed with fear as she started the car and lowered the power windows.

"Is anything wrong?" she asked, hoping he hadn't suddenly changed his mind.

Anthony's left arm was draped casually over the steering wheel, and she could hear the low hum of old R & B music playing.

"No. I just wanted to let you know that if you ever did land in jail for trespassing, I would bail you out."

She tilted her head, feeling a little self-conscious. "Oh really, why?"

Even at a distance, his gaze was so strong that the intensity in his eyes felt palpable.

"Just look in the mirror. I would never deny the rest of the world the opportunity to enjoy that killer smile of yours."

Liza kept her eyes on his, grateful for the distance. It made it easier to hide her attraction to him. He couldn't possibly have guessed that she liked him. Could he?

Without waiting for her response, Anthony waved again, backed out and left.

She sat in her truck and replayed the undeniable hint of flirtation in his voice. A pleasurable tremor spun through her body as she thought about what the slightest change in his tone could possibly mean.

He was a beautiful man, perfect in every way, on the outside at least.

Her mother, who had always been obsessed with beauty, had taught her, practically drilled into her head, that men wanted perfection and wouldn't settle for anything else.

What could a cosmetic surgeon, a man who made a living making women look as perfect as they could afford, possibly see in someone like her? Though he'd already seen her scar and while he didn't seem to care, maybe deep down he did, she reasoned to herself.

In her head, she played back her mother's voice, and it was always the same words that threatened to decimate her self-esteem.

He doesn't like you. Not really. He's just being nice.

Liza leaned back against the seat. For the first time in her life, she knew she had a chance to prove that the words of her mother, though she probably meant well, were completely false.

And if they weren't?

She would brush them aside, like she had before.

Maybe Anthony was just being nice, and maybe she'd never have his love. But she could design him a beautiful clinic that would make him remember her forever, and build her own career at the same time.

Her eyes glanced toward her camera. Fantasies of him would just have to be enough.

And maybe, just maybe, they didn't have to be.

With a confident nod, she threw her truck into Reverse, and with a spray of gravel dust, drove away.

Chapter 4

Liza crossed her legs and drummed her fingers on her kneecap, fighting the urge to peek outside the parlor windows or to check her phone again or to scream aloud.

Where was he?

She knew Anthony lived in the new condos at the other end of Magnolia Avenue, the main thoroughfare in town on which the bed-and-breakfast was also located. So he didn't have to travel far, unless of course, he was coming from the hospital.

Maybe there had been some kind of emergency?

Life in a small town like Bay Point meant quiet evenings, though occasionally there were the sounds of people walking by and children running on the sidewalk.

Maisie slapped her magazine against her lap like she was swatting a fly, and Liza jumped at the noise.

"Honey, would you stop being so nervous? You look like you're about to thread your first needle!"

Liza held back a giggle. That Maisie even put the tabloid down was a minor miracle in itself. When she started reading about what she called "her" stars, she did not like to be disturbed. It was the only time the woman shut up.

Maisie pointed a finger. "You're the one who keeps telling me it's not a date."

"And it's not," Liza reaffirmed, hiding a smile. "I'm sorry for being so antsy."

She'd arrived at Maisie's bed-and-breakfast nearly a month ago, and had become quite fond of the charming widow. Since that time, she'd gone from being shy and quiet to almost as talkative as the proprietress herself, but this was one time that she had to hold back.

In her mind, she knew that her meeting with Anthony was not a date, but in her heart, she knew better. She wouldn't admit her growing feelings for him to anyone, not even herself.

Maisie grunted and picked up her magazine once more. "Oh Lord. Now look what you made me do."

She scowled, turning the magazine outward and held it up so Liza could see. "Brad Pitt's got a paper wrinkle right across his crotch."

Liza burst out laughing. She enjoyed spending time with Maisie as much as she could. But tonight, all she wanted to do was escape. The best place would be in Anthony's arms, but she'd settle for a seat next to him at the dinner table.

"I think Brad will survive. After all, he's married to the most beautiful woman in the world."

"You are just as beautiful as her, child. And don't you forget it."

Maisie never minced words, and Liza smiled, basking in the compliment, which she knew was genuine.

"Thank you, but as I said, this is a business meeting. That's all." Liza shrugged. "Besides, I invited him. Not the other way around."

Maisie raised a brow. "Okay. If you say so."

She snapped her magazine open again. "Don't fret about his being late. He's a doctor. They keep their patients and their women waiting. I think it's in their genetic makeup."

Liza decided that she better change the subject. Though she adored Maisie, once she got an idea in her head, there was no stopping her.

She fanned her face with her hand. "Is it warm in here?"

Maisie lowered her magazine. "Not to me. It's too early for you to get hot flashes. So it's probably your nerves about this date that's not a date," she finished with a sly smile.

"Speaking of dates, where's Prentice? Is he going to be paying a visit tonight?"

The elderly security guard worked at City Hall. A former deacon, his penchant for raunchy humor had gotten him kicked out of the local church. Liza learned through the grapevine that he carried his notorious reputation around like a badge of honor.

"Who knows?" Maisie replied, sounding annoyed. "I can't keep up with that man's schedule. I have my own life."

Two can play at this game.

"So he's not your boyfriend, then?" Liza teased.

Maisie laid the magazine on her lap. "He's a distraction."

As Liza roared with laughter, the doorbell rang, and she got up to answer it.

"Sit down," Maisie ordered. "Don't be so rushed to open the door. He'll think you're desperate."

Liza stayed put and grinned at her host's old-fashioned thinking.

Maisie grasped the arm of her chair for balance as she got up. "Plus, I want to see what he looks like before you do."

"Why?" Liza asked suspiciously, watching Maisie neatly lay her magazine on a pile of others. "You already know what he looks like."

"I want to see if he's decent."

She giggled. "What do you think he's going to do? Arrive naked?"

"Lord, let's hope so," Maisie replied, a wicked glint in her eye.

Had the woman gone out of her mind?

A few seconds later, she appeared at the entry of the parlor with the gorgeous Dr. Marbet as her escort.

He bowed, a wry smile on his face. "Maisie told me that you wanted to make sure I was decent."

Liza blushed as Maisie stood there looking innocent. She wanted to throttle the woman for putting her in such an uncomfortable situation.

Anthony was dressed in dark jeans and a cream-colored

shirt that fit his muscular physique perfectly. The look was casual, yet sophisticated.

She cleared her throat. "Um. Yeah. You look fine."
Oh-so-fine.

"Ready to go?" he asked.

Liza caught his eyes watching her as she uncrossed her legs and smoothed her light pink skirt. It was dressy enough for their meeting without being ostentatious.

"In just a few minutes," she replied. "I just need to have a word with Maisie."

Anthony patted Maisie's hand before unlooping his arm from hers. "It was nice seeing you again."

He tipped his head in Liza's direction. "I'll meet you on the porch."

Liza held back a laugh as Maisie turned and appraised Anthony as he walked down the short hallway and out the door.

When he was gone, Maisie toddled into the room, fanning her hand in front of her face. "Give me your arm. I feel like I'm going to faint!"

Liza gave her a grateful hug, and then assisted her to her chair. Maisie had tricked her, but she did feel slightly less nervous.

She grabbed her purse. "Can I get you anything before I leave? Iced tea?"

Maisie shook her head, and with an innocent smile on her face, picked up one of her tabloids.

"Just don't do anything I wouldn't do."

Liza giggled. "It's just a meeting. I'll be back before you know it."

She took one last look in the oval mirror that hung just inside the B and B's foyer.

Tonight she'd chosen to wear her hair down again, out of habit, mainly because it hid her scar. She knew she shouldn't care what Anthony thought about her appearance, but the truth was that she did. Add in the fact that he was a cosmetic surgeon, and she was more self-conscious than normal.

She slowly opened the door and held back a low groan at the sight of Anthony leaning against the porch column, his back to hers. Maybe it was the cut of his jeans, but his rear looked mighty tempting to hold on to, for dear life or pure pleasure.

He turned when she shut the door behind her and gave her a quick hug. She drew in a breath, trying to ignore the shock waves zipping through her body.

"What was that about back there?"

She shrugged. "Oh, just Maisie being Maisie."

He looked down at her bare legs as she walked down the stairs. "How's that ankle?"

Liza felt her face get hot, and she was surprised he remembered her clumsiness.

"Oh, it's fine. Thanks."

He pursed his lips. "With those shoes you're wearing tonight, I would hope so."

At his playful tone, she looked down at her toes. On a whim, she'd decided to wear heels instead of flats, even though she felt like she was going to take a tumble with every step.

"If I do end up in the emergency room, at least I

won't have to wait all night to see a doctor. I'll have one right by my side," she quipped with a smile.

Anthony took his keys out of his pocket, and she raised a brow at the mischievous grin on his face.

She had assumed that they would go to Lucy's Bar and Grille. It was close, casual, and the only restaurant in town. But not for long.

Mayor Langston's extensive redevelopment plan was encouraging more people to choose downtown Bay Point as the location for their small business. As a result, several new restaurants were slated to open in the next few months. Although Lucy's was well loved, everyone was looking forward to having more local dining choices.

"You do know that we could just walk there," she teased, noticing his truck idling at the curb. After the shadow of confusion in his eyes, she asked, "We *are* going to Lucy's right?"

Anthony shook his head. "I have something different in mind. Are you up for an adventure?"

Liza hitched in a breath at the feel of his hand cupping the small of her back and knew she could easily get used to his gentle touches.

"Yes," she blurted. "As long as food is involved. I'm starved."

Anthony grinned. "Food and more."

She raised a brow, perplexed at his comment, and his smile widened.

"Let me help you. I'd rather not ruin our evening together with a trip to the hospital."

He kept his hand on the small of her back as he

guided her down the steps and over the aging redbrick front path. He opened the door for her and waited until she was safely inside.

As he rounded the truck, Liza looked toward the B and B and saw the edge of the parlor room curtain fall back into place.

If it were anyone else other than Maisie, she would have been annoyed at the intrusion, but it felt good to have someone watching out for her.

Maisie reminded Liza a little of her grandmother. Her overbearing nature was often mistaken for lack of faith in others, when in reality she just didn't want anyone she cared about getting hurt.

Anthony got in, started the car, and cranked up the air conditioning. He put his hands on the steering wheel and turned to her. She noticed how his upper lip was a bit fuller than his lower and decided she liked it.

"Do you mind the change in plans?"

Liza was starting to love her new hometown, and she also enjoyed seeing new places.

"Not at all. I'll try anything once."

As long as I'm with you.

He looked in his side-view mirror before pulling away from the curb and easing onto Magnolia Avenue.

"Good. I wanted to go somewhere more private. There are some people in town who don't agree with what I'm trying to build here, and I'm not ready to have the details of this project blabbed all over Bay Point."

Liza looked over at him, and her insides tensed. Controversy stirring among the locals before they even broke ground? That wasn't a good sign.

"Who doesn't agree with you building the clinic?"

He exhaled, hands tightening on the steering wheel. "Some of my colleagues at the hospital. They think I should just stay in a managed system like they are going to do for the rest of their lives. But I want more."

She couldn't help but wonder if the "more" also meant a special woman in his life. Then she frowned inwardly, remembering how earlier in the week, he'd hinted that he was recently off the market.

"You don't strike me as the type of man who cares what anyone thinks."

He gave her a sidelong glance. "Let me guess, you think I've got a case of doctor's ego?"

Liza bit her lip, not sure how to answer. He did have a big ego, but she guessed that was to be expected given the level of his success.

She found his confidence attractive, even sexy, which made her interactions with him even more confusing. She had to keep reminding herself that he was a potential business partner and nothing more.

She gave him a reassuring smile. Not that he needed it.

"I never said that. Confidence suits you."

He shrugged. "It's part of the job."

"A necessary evil?" she offered.

He nodded. "As a doctor, I have to be self-assured even under the worst of circumstances."

Liza wasn't about to ask for any further details. She couldn't stand the sight of her own blood, let alone that of others.

"But you're right, I don't care what people think. Most of the time."

The slight hesitance in his voice made her wonder if the opposite could be true.

"It hardly matters anyway," he added. "I've got the backing of people who count. Folks like the mayor and others."

Liza had seen Mayor Langston and his wife, Vanessa, who owned a flower shop called Blooms in Paradise, around town on occasion, though she'd never formally met the couple. Vanessa was pregnant with their first child and looked absolutely radiant. Even from a distance, they had the aura of a couple in love.

She sighed deeply, yearning for that same kind of love for herself.

Anthony turned onto the entrance ramp of Highway 101, which meant they were heading out of Bay Point.

He swiveled his head toward her. "Anything wrong?"

Her cheeks warmed under his quick gaze, and she rubbed her arms.

"I just hope that I'm not overdressed again for wherever we are going."

He glanced over. "Let's see, you've got a skirt, a fancy blouse, heels high enough to trip but low enough for dancing. I'd say you're just about right."

She crossed her legs and smiled. "I'm not going to argue with that diagnosis, Doctor."

"Drop the doctor bit, and we'll have a great time," he said with a grin.

"Okay, *Anthony.* Where are you taking me anyway?" she asked.

"Hold on," he said, as he crooked his arm into the back seat and rummaged around, without taking his eyes off the road.

"Does this give you a hint?"

"A cowboy hat?" She watched him place it onto his head, one-handed. "Where are we going? A rodeo?"

"Would you actually go to a rodeo?"

With you, I'd go anywhere.

But she didn't tell him that. If she did, she could pretty much kiss her chance at the project goodbye. She wanted to earn it based on her talents and experience alone, not on her ability to charm her way into the job.

She shrugged, trying to play it cool. "I'll pretty much try anything once."

"Like commercial design?" he replied.

Liza's breath caught in her throat, and she hugged her small purse to her stomach. She couldn't tell if he was teasing or trying to learn more about her.

"I thought you were okay with the fact none of my commercial designs had ever been built. Has something changed?"

"I don't recall saying that I was okay with it," he said, his tone serious.

Liza felt her heart drop into her stomach. Was he reconsidering her for the role?

"I have no control over what design a client chooses. When I was at my former company, they either didn't pick mine for the reasons we discussed or the deal fell through, not because I don't have the talent."

He touched her thigh briefly. She could feel the heat

from his skin through the thin fabric of her skirt and ripples of pleasure slid down her legs.

"Calm down. It's true that I'm not happy that none of your designs were built. However, I'm willing to let it go. Otherwise, I wouldn't be here with you right now."

She exhaled a breath she didn't realize she was holding, relieved to know that he was willing to look past something that she was powerless to change.

They reached for the air-conditioning knob. Her hand brushed against his, and she felt a jolt of awareness run through her body at their simultaneous touch.

"I'm sorry," she said, jerking her hand back. "I always turn the air conditioner off when I'm driving on the 101."

"Me, too," Anthony said, turning the dial to the off position, before opening the windows.

"I love the smell of the ocean breeze. It makes everything seem so fresh and clean."

He nodded. "Cliffs on one side of the road, the Pacific Ocean on the other, and somehow, I don't feel hemmed in." He glanced over. "You look kind of wild with your hair like that."

Liza frowned, trying to tuck her hair behind her ears, yet she refused to shut the window.

"Is that bad?"

He patted the top of his cowboy hat as if to indicate his own playfulness.

"No. I like it that you aren't overly concerned about your appearance."

She furrowed her brow. "That's an interesting statement coming from someone who specializes in making women beautiful."

"I guess I meant to say that you don't really need to care. You're a natural beauty."

His eyes danced over her, and her body warmed in response. Something electric transpired between them and hung in the air. It buzzed around their heads, and her heart skipped a beat.

Liza smiled and looked away, not knowing how to respond to his compliment. Somehow she knew in the depths of her being that he really thought she was beautiful.

She watched the jagged edges of cliffs roll by as his truck twisted around the curves and bends in the road. About twenty minutes later, they pulled off the highway.

"The Pickled Egg?"

Liza was barely able to suppress a giggle as he rolled up both windows with the push of a button.

Anthony eased his truck into a spot and smiled as he turned off the ignition.

"The name of the restaurant is odd, but somehow it suits this place."

The one-story structure had a weather-beaten look. The wood siding was aged and gray, the tin roof was brown and rusty, and the stairs leading up to the porch sagged in the middle. Foot-tapping bluegrass spilled from the open windows, enhancing its charm.

"The parking lot is packed," she said. "That's always a good sign."

Once inside, a blond-haired hostess greeted them,

and Liza noticed she couldn't keep her eyes off Anthony.

"We'd like a table away from the music, if possible," he said.

"The farthest place would be the patio deck. Is that okay?"

He glanced at Liza, and she nodded in approval. "Lead the way," he instructed.

The restaurant's bar was long, the tables were close together and the music was loud. As they squeezed their way through the packed dance floor, she was glad to see that the customers were a mixed crowd of couples and families.

Many of the women looked up as they made their way to the patio. Maisie had informed her a week ago that Anthony's elusive personality and reputation as America's cosmetic surgeon for the Hollywood elite made him one of the most talked about residents in Bay Point. Even if they didn't know who Anthony was, it was obvious they appreciated his good looks and muscular physique.

She wondered if the cowboy hat, which looked totally adorable on him, also served as a disguise and if he'd chosen the restaurant because it was a place where he wouldn't be recognized.

Liza felt his hand gently grab and hold on to hers, making her feel protected as he led her through a throng of dancers.

Moments later, they stepped out onto the deck and were shown to a table in the corner, which had a fabulous view of the ocean.

Anthony let go of her hand, and they both sat down.

"Two drafts," he said. "Whatever you have on tap."

The waitress nodded, handed them their menus and left.

"How do you know I like beer?"

He grinned. "I don't. Those beers are for me."

Liza opened up her menu. She felt like bopping him over the head with it, and on impulse, she did.

"Don't twist those pretty lips to the side," Anthony said. "I was just kidding. You can have one."

The waitress brought their beers over in two frosty mugs, and they placed their orders.

Anthony held up his mug. "To life, love and bull-dozers."

"That's a strange toast, but okay!" She laughed, and they clinked mugs.

The beer was cold and crisp and tickled her throat as it went down.

"So, what made you choose our little town to build your house?"

She shrugged. "I have a few residential clients in San Francisco and Los Angeles, so the location was ideal."

"And that's all?"

Liza squirmed in her seat. She wasn't ready to get personal with Anthony, even if the temptation to confess every secret she held in her heart was growing stronger each time she was near him.

Could he ever understand how alone she sometimes felt, losing both of her parents in such a short time? How she just needed someone to hold her and tell her that everything was going to be okay?

"The mayor's redevelopment plan has garnered a lot of press over the past several months. I think I moved to Bay Point at the right time."

Anthony took a long pull on his beer and sat back in his chair. "My only fear is that redevelopment and gentrification go hand in hand. I didn't grow up here. I grew up in Miami, and I think you'll agree that the downtown area here is very charming. That's not something we want to lose to big-box retailers and chain restaurants."

He offered her the bread basket that the waitress had just set down.

Liza nodded. "Yes, but when I move into my new house, I'm not sure I'll be hanging around downtown that often."

She picked up a piece of corn bread and buttered it.

"I will say this, I'll take Ruby's coffee any day rather than over-priced stuff that tastes like jet fuel."

He laughed. "Bay Point grows on you. You'll see. The mayor assures me that he's going to do whatever it takes to maintain the small-town feel. You'll meet him when you pitch your design."

Though she had just swallowed a piece of the corn bread, it felt like it was stuck in her throat. She took a couple of sips of beer.

"The mayor will be there?"

"Yes, I invited him because I value his opinion. He's actually become a good friend of mine, and I try to go to his wife's flower shop as often as I can."

Liza felt her insides churn with disappointment. A man going to a flower shop often could only mean one thing: he had a girlfriend. She was dying to confirm, but doing so would open her up for the same line of questioning, so she decided to keep her mouth shut.

"I'm glad you support small businesses."

"I'm about to be a small-business owner myself, though not for long."

"What do you mean?"

"If things go well, and I am fully expecting that they will, I want to franchise the clinic into other areas of California, and ultimately, nationwide."

Liza felt her eyes widen. If Anthony was going to franchise the clinic, her design would be replicated, too, making the opportunity to work with him more appealing than ever.

"That's terrific news. Now that I know you want to franchise, it will help me better plan the architectural design from the very beginning. I can make sure it will work in any area of the country."

Anthony smiled. "Then I'm glad I brought it up. It's not something I've discussed with anyone else other than my business partners."

Her palms tingled with excitement. If she was the only one who knew that valuable piece of information, it meant she had an advantage over the firms that were pitching designs for the clinic.

Why did he decide to tell her and not her competitors? She wasn't about to ask.

The waitress set down their orders: a pulled pork sandwich and French fries for her, and a rib eye steak for Anthony. They were just about to dig in when a woman appeared at their table.

"Hello, Dr. Marbet. Remember me?"

The woman was clearly drunk, smelling of whiskey and looking unsteady on her super-high platform heels. She looked familiar, like Liza had seen her on television or in a bit part from a movie.

She put her hands on their table, and Liza was shocked when, without waiting for an answer from Anthony, she leaned in close to him and practically shoved her large boobs in his face.

"After all these years, these babies are still holding up," she announced, cupping her breasts.

She turned to Liza, who hid a smile at the woman's outrageous behavior.

"This man saved my bustline and my marriage."

With the woman's attention diverted, Liza watched as Anthony took the opportunity to move his chair back, ever so slightly.

"You his wife?" the woman slurred.

Liza was so shocked at the question she couldn't speak.

"You're a lucky woman. Dr. Marbet has some very skilled hands."

Without another word, the woman staggered away and went back inside.

"That was…interesting," Liza said, with a wry grin. "Does that happen to you often?"

"Actually, it doesn't. Most people like to keep their cosmetic surgery private."

He glanced at the open door leading to the restaurant and shook his head.

"Others don't. I'm glad she didn't stick around. I've had so many patients over the years that I really don't remember her name. I do remember that she's an actress, and a pretty bad one."

Liza laughed. "From the way she's been drinking, she probably doesn't remember her name either."

She clucked her tongue at him. "She thought I was your wife."

Anthony grinned, picked up a knife and cut into his steak. "Maybe she thinks we're a cute couple?"

She popped a fry into her mouth and chewed, pondering his response.

"And what if she does?"

Anthony leaned his elbows on the table and laughed. "She'd be right. Think you can keep up with me, my dreams of grandeur *and* my cowboy hat?"

Liza's heart raced at his flirtatious challenge. "Perhaps," she responded, playing along.

When they finished their meal, he got up and extended his hand toward her. "Care to join me in a dance to work off all these calories? I hate making a fool of myself alone."

Liza told herself that it was only the sound of the infectious music that got her out of her chair rather than the chance to be close to him.

She took his hand and locked her eyes with his.

"It's been a while," she cautioned as he led her inside. "And bluegrass was never my thing."

Anthony slipped his arms around her waist and pulled her close.

"What happened to the woman who would try anything once?"

Liza looked up at him, and when their eyes met, her lips quivered.

"She hasn't gone anywhere. She's right here. In your arms."

His grin seemed to stretch ear-to-ear, and zoomed straight to her heart.

He took her hand in his. "Then let's get to it!"

The boot-skipping rhythm had their feet moving, even as they laughingly tried to keep from stepping on each other's toes. Out of the corner of her eye, she saw the other dancers move out of the way to allow the clumsy couple some more room.

Anthony bent down, his lips grazing her ear, sending a thousand tingles down her spine.

"Not as easy as the Electric Slide, is it? I think I've stepped on your feet more than you've stepped on mine."

Liza shook her head. "No. Your dancing is fine."

She took a quick glance around the room, and it seemed like they were the center of attention. "However, we may be making a spectacle of ourselves."

"Perhaps we are," he said low in her ear. "Who cares?"

Anthony pulled her even closer, and her breasts became instantly aroused. She laid her head against his shoulder, inhaling the scent of him percolating through his shirt.

Crisp sandalwood. Simmering heat.

As they rocked and swayed together to the music, the strength of his embrace and his own physical reaction to her signaled that something had changed between them. And she wasn't sure she could handle it.

Her heart pumped wildly in her chest, and she worried what would happen if she began to care about *him* too much.

He tilted her chin up with the tip of his finger, and leaned in close to her face.

His full lips were tempting enough to kiss, to bite. Did she want to? *Yes.*

Did she dare?

His face blurred out of focus as he lowered his chin, blending his lips with hers.

Her eyes slid shut as she relaxed into the feel of his soft lips on hers. Tender and sweet, making her smile inside. Still swaying together, slower now, he pulled her closer, and she could feel his desire.

The room seemed to fade away. All that mattered was now, this moment with Anthony. His mouth so hot, his tongue probing her own, and the helpless sense that she was falling into him, into something she couldn't control.

She moaned, knowing that the sound of her pleasure was hidden beneath the harsh twang of the music, but he'd felt it. The vibrations of her need. His fingers stroked her cheek lightly, as if to draw her into him. Into a place all their own.

Somewhere she could lose herself.

She pulled away, before the song could end, before she would beg him to never, ever stop. He released her, and she wished she were back in his arms.

"What's wrong?" he asked.

"I need some air," she replied, in a voice sharper than she intended.

"Can you take me home please?"

"Yeah." The hurt in his voice was subtle. "I'll find the waitress and pay the check. Meet me in the parking lot."

Liza went back to the patio for her purse. She breathed a sigh of relief that it was actually there. Though she had hidden it under the table, leaving her personal belongings in a strange place was just another sign that she was in over her head.

The deck had a separate exit, so she took it, thankful she could avoid the crowd inside.

It wasn't until they were back at the bed-and-breakfast that Anthony spoke. He pulled in front, turned off the car and glanced over at her.

"What happened back there, Liza?"

Though it was difficult, she met his eyes.

"I was having fun," she admitted. "Then we started acting like a couple of potential lovers, not potential business partners, and…"

Her voice fell away, and she looked out the closed window.

"It wasn't fun anymore?" he said, his tone slightly mocking. "That's not how I read things."

Liza turned back, her eyes flashing.

"Oh? And how did you read things?"

Anthony's hands tensed, but his shoulders slumped a bit.

"I didn't mean to offend you."

He glanced over at her, and his eyes roamed hers.

"You're right. Let's set the record straight. Neither of us should read anything into this."

His words cut straight to her heart. Like so many times before, she'd already gone down the path of a relationship before there was even a hint that one existed.

Liza was shocked when Anthony got out and walked with her to the front door. He was a true gentleman. She was about to retrieve the keys from her purse when he touched her hand.

"Wait. I owe you an apology."

She swallowed hard. "What for?"

His eyes roamed her body again, heating her up in all the right places.

"I'm sorry the kiss couldn't last longer."

Chapter 5

Anthony sank back into his leather recliner, wiggled his bare toes and let out a slow breath. This was the first time he'd been off his feet in over twenty-four hours, and it felt like heaven.

He leaned his head back and closed his eyes. "Now, if I only had a good woman in my lap, I'd be in paradise."

The only one he'd even consider fulfilling that fantasy with was Liza. Just the thought of her luscious lips upon his and her equally luscious backside sliding against his thighs, both of them naked, made him groan.

He slipped his shirt over his head and tossed it on the floor.

After dancing with her at The Pickled Egg and seeing how good she felt in his arms, talking to her was no longer enough. Not only did he want her in his lap, he wanted her in his bed.

His mind captured the visual of the two of them making love in his favorite chair and held on. He found it difficult to let go of it.

Too bad she didn't want the same thing, he thought, rubbing the heel of his hand against his temple.

After several restless nights where he'd woken up hard as a rock and needing release and not getting it, he realized she had been right to pull away.

He liked Liza. A lot. But there was no way he was going to lift his personal ban on workplace romance. The clinic was too important.

Dazed by her beauty and a couple of beers that night, he would have carried her out of the restaurant and had her in the backseat of his truck, like a couple of teenagers, if she'd let him.

Good thing she was more in control of herself than he was.

Even more reason why he knew he should go against Doc Z's request and hire a twenty-person architectural firm instead of the beautiful woman who had captured his mind and stimulated his body.

Tomorrow was Liza's presentation to him and his board of directors. He drummed his fingers on the leather armrest in anticipation of her proposed designs.

He couldn't wait to see them, couldn't wait to see her, and because of her, he'd felt alive for the first time in a long while.

Anthony frowned, knowing that she had no idea what she was about to walk into the next day.

He reached for a tumbler of bourbon and took a long drink. The liquid burned all the way down and ebbed away the physical effects of his desire.

Settling back in his chair, he flicked on the television to his favorite sports network.

He flipped through the channels and found a basketball game that was just starting. He didn't care what team was playing or how they ranked, pro or college, just as long as they played hard enough to erase his thoughts of the hospital, his clinic and Liza.

Hours later, Anthony awoke with a start and squinted at the screen. While he slept, the college game he'd started watching had morphed into a pro game. The doorbell was ringing incessantly. He grabbed his cell and quickly navigated to his security app and selected video intercom.

"About time you answered," Doc Z said, mugging the camera.

What was Doc doing in Bay Point?

Anthony jerked his arms back into his shirt.

"Sorry, I'll be right there."

He closed the app and straggled out of his chair. Before opening the door, he grabbed the tumbler of bourbon just to have something to hold on to.

As soon as he opened the door, he propped his arm against the jamb, so that he wouldn't slide to the tile floor. He was so sleep deprived that when he woke up, he felt like he'd been run over by a truck.

"Surprise!" Doc Z exclaimed.

"Indeed it is," Anthony replied, rubbing the sleep from his eyes.

"I was on my way to visit a lady friend in Utah and decided to make a pit stop."

Even in the twilight, he could see the twinkle in his friend's eye.

Anthony twisted his lips into a smirk. "You're about a thousand miles out of your way."

Doc Z guffawed. "I am, aren't I? She can wait. Besides, you told me your door was always open."

"I said that back in med school, and I meant my dorm room," he said, wryly, stifling a yawn.

Doc Z wagged a finger in his face and picked up his suitcase. "Let me in, and I'll tell you why I had to disturb your beauty sleep."

Once Doc was inside, Anthony closed the door and leaned against it.

"Why didn't you let me know you were coming into town? I would have picked you up at the airport."

"I rented a car." Doc Z set down his suitcase. "But you can make it up to me by pouring me more than a thimbleful of the same stuff you've got in your hand."

Anthony strode over to the small bar, retrieved a glass and filled it halfway.

Doc took it, swallowed and grinned, before strolling into the living room.

"This is so good it should be outlawed."

Anthony folded his arms. "I'm glad to see you. I really am, but why are you here all of a sudden?"

"Oh, just seeing the sights. I've heard Bay Point is a beautiful town with beautiful women." He gestured toward the television with his glass. "Good game?"

"I wouldn't know. I slept through it." Anthony muted

the sound. "So, why don't you tell me why you're really here?"

Doc finished his drink, and then peered through the empty glass. "To see all the beautiful women, why else?" he said, sounding a bit offended.

"There are beautiful women in Utah," Anthony replied. "You wouldn't happen to be checking up on Liza?"

Doc Z sat down on the leather sofa with a grunt and ran his hand over his smooth coffee-colored bald head. He had an innocent look on his bearded face, but Anthony wasn't fooled.

"Now, where would you get an idea like that?"

"Because I know how you are," Anthony insisted. "You're an overgrown mother hen."

Doc scanted his eyes at him, and then pointed to his empty glass to signal he wanted a refill.

"Father Hen."

"So, what if I am? Liza is like a daughter to me, as much as you're like a son."

Anthony raised a brow, and while he appreciated his kind words, he wasn't going to let Doc off the hook. "And you're like a father to me. But Liza—"

"Won't even know that I'm here."

Doc tapped the rim of the glass with his thumb, and gave Anthony the stare-down. "What does a man have to do to get another drink in this place?"

Anthony ignored his request and wondered what Liza would think if she knew they were linked by this one man. He realized he could probably learn a lot about the woman by talking to Doc, but he decided to just leave curiosity aside and focus on the big picture.

His clinic.

"How are you going to manage that? Bay Point is a very small town."

Doc steepled his fingers. "Liza's presentation is tomorrow. You give her the gig a few days later, as we discussed, and I'll be on a plane to see my girl in Salt Lake City."

"Just like that?" Anthony said, not bothering to chase away the doubt in his voice.

"Yep, just like that. It's as easy as pouring me another drink," Doc said, handing Anthony his glass.

"What if I told you that I'm starting to have second thoughts?"

"About giving me a refill?" Doc Z said, eyeing him carefully. "I'm perfectly capable of getting it myself."

"No, about Liza," Anthony responded, trying to stay patient. Sometimes he wondered if Doc tried his nerves on purpose.

When he was teaching med school, Doc would never accept an incomplete answer from any student in his class, and yet, he gave them all the time.

Doc settled back in his seat. "What was Liza's reaction to the build site?"

"She fell in love with it."

"I knew she would," he said in a triumphant tone. "You can't call things off now."

Anthony strode to the bar. "What do you mean? Of course I could."

"Sure, if you want to break the girl's heart."

Though spoken gently, Doc's words hit him like a bullet. He remembered how her eyes had lit up at the view of the Pacific Ocean, and how animated she seemed as they toured the grounds, talking about the possibilities.

Lastly, he recalled the feel of his lips on hers, and the kiss that he couldn't forget.

Break Liza's heart? That was the last thing Anthony wanted.

He set down Doc's tumbler, grabbed the nearly empty bottle of bourbon and swirled it around as if that would give him the answer. With a disgusted sigh, he poured the rest of the liquid into the glass, walked over and handed it back to his friend.

"We've got to tell her the truth, Doc."

"Uh-huh," Doc grunted, then swallowed. "No way."

"Why not?" Anthony demanded.

"We can't. Not yet anyway. Besides, even if she did know, I doubt she'd turn down the job. You know she really wants it."

And I want her. Badly, Anthony thought, which was deliciously tempting and potentially disastrous for both of them.

"Yes, I know," he admitted.

"So what do you have to lose?" Doc asked. "Besides one of the best architects and one of the best people I've ever known?"

Anthony leaned against the bar. "You're really not making this easy."

Doc downed the rest of his drink and smacked his lips. "Have I ever?"

"Truth," Anthony admitted with a resigned grin. "Consider it done."

With a wide grin, Doc Z walked over and clapped Anthony on his shoulder. The gesture, while fatherly, could only mean trouble.

"So, until I get a joyous call from Liza, and since you want me to stay out of sight, I guess, I'll be bunking here for a few days."

"Heaven help the both of us," Anthony joked as he picked up Doc's suitcase and headed for the guest bedroom.

Chapter 6

Liza opened one eye, squinted at the alarm clock and rolled over. She'd spent the past several weeks nailing down an architectural design she thought best fit Anthony's vision for his cosmetic surgery clinic. Countless hours of work and more than a few sleepless nights would culminate in the most important presentation of her career.

She stared at the floral wallpaper in her room, and her stomach clenched with fear.

How many times had she come up with amazing designs that were never actually brought to life? Her bosses always advised her to not take it personally, but having her work rejected always hurt. It would hurt even more if the rejection came from Anthony.

What if he hates them?

Liza twirled a lock of hair that had escaped from her rollers sometime during the night. She wouldn't think about that right now. Those what-if kinds of thoughts were paralyzing, and a darn good reason to stay in bed all day with a cup of tea and a good book.

She kicked off the covers with her feet and hopped out of bed before she could change her mind. She walked to the antique mirror in the corner of her small quarters.

"This will be my best presentation ever," she said aloud and with as much confidence as she could muster with her morning breath.

Liza took a leisurely shower and slipped into her most expensive suit, custom-made by a designer in Chicago. Wearing it always made her feel like she could conquer the world.

An hour later, she packed up her laptop and her portfolio case, grabbed her purse and headed downstairs. She'd chosen a room on the third floor of the bed-and-breakfast primarily for the privacy, plus, she was able to negotiate a fair price on a long-term rental.

Though it was still early, she could hear dishes clanking and the nasal sound of a boisterous talk radio program. The scent of eggs and bacon hit her nostrils before she even reached the first floor.

"How can anyone sleep around here with all these delicious smells?" Liza declared, a big smile on her face as she entered the room.

Maisie turned in her place and her eyes widened. "What a sharp suit! You look like you're about to go on the air!"

"More like on the chopping block," Liza quipped as Maisie toddled over to her.

"Don't be nervous, honey. In that fancy suit, you'll have that cute doctor under your spell in no time. I saw the way he looked at you that night he picked you up for dinner."

When Liza opened her mouth in protest, Maisie waggled a finger. "And don't tell me again that it was just a business meeting," she added. "Because we both know that it wasn't."

Liza's face warmed, and not from the heat in the small room.

"You're right," she said, setting her things on an empty chair. "But it's not just Anthony that I have to impress today, Maisie, it's a whole team of people."

"Like whom?" Maisie said, putting her hands on her hips.

"Mayor Langston, for one. I don't know who else will be there."

"Gregory? Oh, don't worry about him. He's a lot less uptight since he got married."

She pursed her lips. "Just don't mention the carousel."

Liza frowned. "Why not? Isn't it safe?"

Maisie moved past her and picked up a pair of tongs. "Oh, the city has done a lot of improvements to it, both cosmetic and mechanically, in the past year so it's definitely safe. Just not for hearts."

"What do you mean?" Liza asked, curious now.

She lifted the bacon out of the pan, put each strip on a paper towel–covered plate to drain and turned back.

"There's a saying around town that if you ride the carousel with your sweetheart you'll fall in love. It's one of a few interesting legends in Bay Point."

A few, Liza thought, wondering what the others were.

"Romantic, isn't it?" Maisie continued with a wink. "At least, to those folks who are in love or want to be in love."

In love or want to be in love? That certainly did not describe her, she thought, as her face warmed a second time. She knew she was lying to herself. It's not that she didn't love being in love. But in her experience, on the other side of elation there was only pain. Joy was short-lived, and for her, the risk was too great, especially with Anthony.

"Is that what happened to the mayor?"

Maisie nodded. "Big time. Just after he was reelected for a second term. Oh, he grumbles about the carousel from time to time when he gets teased," she grinned, knowingly. "But he and Vanessa are so happy."

Liza was dying to ask more questions, but she didn't dare. The woman already suspected there was more than business to her relationship with Dr. Marbet.

Her heart clenched in her chest. She knew the truth.

It was lodged in the whirlwind of passionate kisses that she'd abruptly ended, and that he'd implied he didn't want to end.

So who was right? And who was wrong?

She couldn't blame him. He was so used to being desired by women that he just assumed she did, too. And while it was true that she did desire him, if only for one night, she wasn't willing to risk the best opportunity she had for establishing her architectural business in Bay Point and Northern California at large.

She shook her head. One night could destroy a life-time of dreams.

Maisie set a plate down on the table and gave her an odd look. "Why are you shaking your head? Sit down and have some breakfast."

Liza gave her a weak smile, and laid her hand on her stomach. "Oh, I couldn't possibly eat. I'm too nervous."

During her time at the bed-and-breakfast, Liza had noticed that none of Maisie's plates matched. This one had a rooster in the middle of it, beak taunted open, like it was ready to swallow any food that was put upon it. Maisie put down a stainless-steel fork and a knife next to it that looked like they'd been bought at a flea market—charming, vintage and very dull.

"Even more reason to get some food in there to calm it down."

"I don't want to get my suit dirty," she insisted. "With my luck, I'll spill something on it."

Maisie put her hands on Liza's shoulders and guided her to a chair. "Not to worry, honey, I've got just the thing."

Liza sat down, watching in patient amusement as Maisie went over to what, with all the clanging and rustling, was probably a junk drawer. Her amusement turned to horror at what Maisie held proudly in her hands.

An adult-sized bib.

Liza arose from her chair slowly. She wouldn't be caught dead wearing that thing, even inside, where no one could see her. She picked up her belongings and eased toward the door.

"The meeting will be over in an hour or so. Let's have breakfast when I return," she suggested. "I can change and neither of us will have to worry about getting my suit messed up."

Maisie shrugged and tied the bib around her own neck. "Suit yourself. Bacon is never good reheated."

She gave her a hug. "I'll be back soon. Wish me luck?"

"I don't believe in luck, but I believe in you." Maisie hugged her back. "How's that?"

"That's the best advice I've heard in a long time."

Liza smiled as she went out the door, her nerves oddly calm.

The streets and sidewalks were wet, but the moisture was already disappearing, warmed out of existence by the morning sun.

She'd slept so soundly she hadn't even heard the rain on the roof, and she realized it was the first night she hadn't had a dream about Anthony. It was probably a sign that her subconscious mind was processing what her heart already knew.

As much as they were attracted to each other, in the end, business relationships that turned sexual often ended badly. It would be better for both of them if she kept focused on her goals, rather than how his lips made her feel.

The distance to Anthony's condo, where they would gather in a special meeting room, was short, but would still allow her some time to review her presentation in her head.

But as she made her way down Magnolia Avenue, she found that her mind drew a blank. She couldn't think of anything but making sure she put one foot in front of the other, without falling flat on her face.

Liza walked past two new restaurants that were in the process of being constructed and a few new stores that had already opened, including a tiny, independent bookstore.

Although moving here was risky, Bay Point was in the midst of an exciting turnaround, and Liza was hopeful that she would be able to play an important role in the town's rebirth.

A few minutes later, she arrived at the condo's community center. She quickly found the meeting room located on the first floor. The door was open, but she stood aside from it, where she couldn't be seen, and took a deep breath.

Liza grasped the handles of her laptop case, portfolio and purse tightly and entered the room. Anthony had his back to her and was speaking to someone she did not recognize.

When he was done, he turned around and walked toward her. To her surprise, his eyes lit up.

"Liza! Welcome. It's good to have you with us this morning."

"It's great to be here, Dr. Marbet."

She knew instinctively to refer to him by his proper name rather than Anthony, and would not even think of embarrassing him.

She shook his hand, and he let go quickly, and her eyes averted from his lips.

The other individuals in the room had no idea that they'd kissed, that she'd felt the evidence of his desire pressed up against her.

Liza took another deep breath as she followed him over to a table in front of the room.

"We've got a projector and monitor set up. Just don't ask me if I know how to use it. I'm all thumbs when it comes to that type of technology."

She smiled politely. "It's a good thing you're not all thumbs when it comes to surgery."

Anthony laughed. "Let me introduce you to the folks around the table."

"This man is a second-rate comedian but a first-rate politician, Mayor Gregory Langston."

"Pleasure to meet you, Liza."

She put down her things and shook his outstretched hand. "I've seen you and your wife around town. It's great to meet you in person."

"These other two individuals are my friends and members of our board of directors, Miss Eloise Bradshaw and Mr. Jack Warren."

"Dr. Marbet has told us all about you," Eloise said in a tone that had Liza wondering exactly what she meant.

Mr. Warren stood and leaned over the table to shake her hand. He had a slight build, but his voice was powerful. "Looking forward to seeing your designs, Miss Sinclair."

Anthony turned to her. "Liza, we'll give you a few minutes to get set up while I get a second cup of coffee."

"I'll join you," Eloise declared, looping her arm through Anthony's in a way that made Liza wonder if the woman was investing more than just her money in Dr. Marbet. Perhaps she was the reason he was off the market? But if he was, then why did he kiss her?

Liza turned away from the conference table and found that her hands were shaking.

She hooked up her computer to the projector, and turned both machines on, then navigated to her presentation. Then she removed her rendering from the portfolio case, and placed it backwards on the stanchion to be revealed at the appropriate time.

Anthony and Eloise reentered the room holding two steaming cups of coffee.

When they were both seated, Anthony said, "Let's get started, shall we? We're all very busy, and while I'm off duty today, there's always a chance I'll get called to the hospital for an emergency."

Liza caught Anthony's eye, and at his nod, she began. "Thank you all for being here today and for allowing me the chance to present my architectural design for Dr. Marbet's cosmetic surgery clinic."

She smiled and clicked to the first slide in her presentation. "Good design is focused on the experience of the customer. This is especially critical in a healthcare setting, where a patient or potential patient is already nervous or anxious about the disease, condition or illness they are trying to get treated."

The next slide showed two arrows in opposite directions and stock photos of attractive people looking confused.

"Wayfinding is critical. Oftentimes, the structure and layout of a building can add another dimension to their overall experience. It's really important that people can find where they are going, which shouldn't be too much of an issue at the clinic because of its smaller footprint."

"Agreed," Jack interjected, holding up a pen in the air. "I have the hardest time finding offices at our hospital. The building is large and the signage is awful."

"It's a known issue in many hospitals around the country," Liza acknowledged, grateful that someone was engaged in the discussion, even if it wasn't Anthony. He had a stony look on his face as if he were distracted.

She took a deep breath. "My design takes into consideration the patient experience, the smaller square footage of the clinic, its beautiful location off the Pacific Coast Highway and much more."

Liza stepped away from her laptop to the stanchion and flipped her rendering over. "This is a design that I call 'Serenity.' We'll dive into the 3-D version on my laptop in a moment, but I just wanted you to see the sketch first."

Miss Bradshaw gasped. "You drew that…by hand?"

"Of course she did," Dr. Marbet said in a tone that sounded half amazed and half scolding. "Architecture *is* art."

Liza nodded. "I always do my sketches first by hand, and once I'm happy with it, I use 3-D software to bring it to life."

She grabbed a pen, which also doubled as a pointer.

"Dr. Marbet's clientele is ninety percent female, so I made the exterior design contemporary and chic. It's soft without being too girly, yet modern enough so that a male patient does not feel embarrassed for being there."

"The redbrick, circular driveway and expansive, covered entry at the front welcome patients, setting the stage for a positive experience."

Anthony cleared his throat. "As you know, I have high-profile patients who want extreme privacy. How have you solved for that?"

She pointed to another area of the rendering. "There is a gated entrance on this side of the building, just for that purpose."

"Very well. How many patient rooms are there?"

Liza warmed at the pleased tone of Anthony's voice. He sounded as if he were happy with the design thus far.

"There are ten patient rooms, ten recovery rooms and three surgical units," she responded, pointing to the corresponding sections of the rendering. "The recovery rooms and a portion of the waiting room have views of the ocean."

"My wife and I have visited the location," Mayor Langston said. "If there's any way you could preserve the natural vegetation of the land, that would be wonderful."

Liza nodded. "We'll be using environmentally friendly building materials, and I have already contacted a landscape designer who is familiar with the plants, flowers and trees that are native to the area."

Eloise lifted her hand and wove it through her long blond locks. "It's a beautiful design. Simply stunning.

I love how open and unassuming it appears, at least, from the outside."

"Thank you, Mrs. Bradshaw."

"It's Miss," she corrected.

Liza nodded and watched as Eloise skirted her eyes at Anthony, making Liza wonder about the true nature of their relationship.

She ignored the sinking feeling in her stomach and walked over to her laptop. "If I could direct your attention to the screen, let me take you through a 3-D tour inside the clinic."

Over the next half hour, she showed them the waiting room, a greenhouse-style atrium, an open-air café, the patient and recovery rooms, and one of the surgical units.

The entire time, Eloise and Jack had offered up more questions than compliments.

Mayor Langston listened attentively, yet also seemed a bit distracted.

But it was Anthony who was cause for concern. Other than his earlier enthusiasm, he stayed silent throughout the presentation. A strange tension filtered through the room, although nobody seemed to notice it but her.

"I've even increased the square footage of your office, Dr. Marbet," she offered, hoping to break the ice and maybe untie the corkscrew knot in her stomach. "No more parking lot. You've got a view of the ocean, too!"

Jack sighed and his whole body seemed to shudder.

"The good doctor's got enough of an ego. Don't feed into it, Miss Sinclair," he advised.

Eloise turned toward him. "I'm sure he'll let you visit from time to time, Jack. We all know how small *your* office is," she said in a playful tone.

"Hey. I want to visit, too!" Mayor Langston piped in. "I'm in public service. My office is a broom closet."

His words seemed to rouse Anthony and he laughed. Then, for the first time in over thirty minutes, he addressed Liza.

"All jokes aside, your design is impressive and very much aligned with my vision. I appreciate your attention to detail. But how much is all of this going to cost me?"

Liza clicked to another slide. "I've done a preliminary cost analysis, taking into consideration construction costs in this area. With careful planning and management, I believe we can complete this project within your budget."

She watched Anthony's face carefully, but he remained stoic and silent as he viewed the screen.

Eloise snorted in disgust. "That cost projection seems really high. Can't we build the clinic with a cheaper budget than that?"

"Of course, one could always go cheaper with anything," Liza replied patiently. "These prices reflect the cost of building 'green,' sourcing environmentally friendly materials and equipment, and acquiring the necessary certifications to achieve LEED status."

"It's like buying organic," Mayor Langston said. "It's good for you, but it's more labor-intensive to grow vegetables without chemicals, so the consumer pays the price."

Anthony stood and walked over to the rendering.

"I told Liza how important it is that we be mindful of the environment with this project, Eloise. I'm glad she proactively incorporated the costs into the budget."

Liza felt her heart skip a beat at his words. He'd praised and defended her at the same time.

"Still, it's going to be extremely important that we monitor our finances," Jack added. "If we plan to franchise the clinic someday, we can't be so overly extravagant that a physician wouldn't want to open up one of their own someday."

"Agreed," Anthony said. "High-end but not so much that a prospective franchisee would have to sell his soul to the devil in order to buy into the business."

He turned back to Liza. "Do you have any other designs to show us?"

Her cheeks flushed, and she shook her head. "No. I had started some other concepts but kept returning to 'Serenity,' so I decided to devote myself to fleshing this one out completely."

Anthony smiled, and it seemed genuine. "I think that was a smart move, and the amount of effort you put into this presentation really shows."

He glanced at his colleagues. "Anybody else have any other questions?"

Liza paused a beat until she was sure no one was going to address her.

"Thanks again for your time, everyone. And if you

select me as your architect, I promise I'll be a hundred percent devoted to this project from start to finish."

She distributed her business card, and then quickly packed up her things while the rest of the group stayed seated.

"I'll walk you to the door."

He appeared distracted again and almost in a hurry to get her out of the room.

Though he maintained a respectable distance, she could almost feel the heat simmering between them as he shook her hand and gently let it go.

"I'll be in touch soon with my decision."

She fully expected to see the next candidates for the interview in the hall. Even though Anthony hadn't told her when the other architects would be presenting, it seemed logical that they would all pitch their designs on the same day.

But when she exited the meeting room, the hall was eerily empty.

Liza frowned. She'd hoped to meet her rivals face-to-face. She might have recognized a few of them from industry conferences or other pitches. Anthony would only have considered the best firms in the country for his project.

Maybe they'd presented earlier in the week, she told herself as she walked outside. She lifted her arm to cover her eyes from the bright morning sun as they adjusted from the previous dim surroundings.

Or perhaps they were running late, which was always a way to irritate people. She hated being late or waiting for people who were.

She gave herself an imaginary pat on the back, glad that the presentation was over. There were only two possibilities now. She would either land the project and be able to advance her own vision for her new life in Bay Point or she wouldn't and her plans would come to a screeching halt. Only temporarily, though, until she figured out a Plan B.

In either case, she wasn't sure how she would ever forget the feeling of standing before Anthony and talking about the one thing that stirred her passions almost as much as he did: architecture.

Liza inhaled a deep breath and almost swooned from the salty air, fighting the urge to run down to the beach, which was only a block or two away.

All she wanted to do was dive into the ocean and swim until she couldn't feel her body anymore. Maybe then, her desire for Dr. Anthony Marbet would be gone, too.

One step at a time. I need to get the gig first.

The mix of exhilaration and fear about all the unknowns she was facing in Bay Point was heady, and at that moment, she could only compare it to her growing feelings for him, which, if left unchecked, could quickly spiral out of control.

Chapter 7

From what Liza had heard, there wasn't a person in town who didn't fear for his or her life walking down the wooden stairs to Bay Point Beach. There was an almost identical set of new stairs being built several yards away, but the project wasn't finished yet.

The sooner the better, she thought as she held onto the railing and dodged weak areas of the structure, thanks to tips from seasoned locals.

Last night, she'd been overjoyed to receive a text from Anthony asking her to meet him on the pier.

But now, her stomach was a tornado of nerves.

She knew the only reason he would meet with her would be to let her know that he'd made a decision. And on a Saturday morning at 8 a.m., when she'd normally be buried deep within the covers of her comfy bed, the news had better be good.

She'd lain awake for a few nights wondering why he'd remained mostly silent during her presentation, giving his investors and the mayor free rein to ask questions. She'd turned over a variety of scenarios in her head, but then decided to let it go. She'd deal with the outcome, whether positive or negative, in her own way, and in her own time.

When she got to the last step, Liza breathed a sigh of relief, removed her sandals and dug her toes into the warm sand.

The beach was empty, except for a young couple walking a very wet golden retriever on the shoreline. Occasionally, the man would toss a tennis ball. The dog would bark and run into the water, and trot back with the ball in his mouth and what Liza swore was a smile of satisfaction on his muzzle.

She arrived at the pier, which had seemed farther away than it actually was, and Anthony was already there. His arms rested loosely on top of the wooden railing as he leaned against it, looking every bit as relaxed in the sunlight as she was nervous.

She slipped her sandals back on her feet. Behind her sunglasses, her eyes widened as she approached him. It had been a long time since she'd seen a man look so good in a pair of wet swim trunks. The material clung like second skin to his round buttocks. Water pooled at his bare feet.

She avoided the small puddle and slid into place next to him. The air seemed to hang between them like a cloud. The heat from his muscled arms radiated outward and grazed hers like a gentle breeze.

"Dogs have all the fun, don't they?"

He turned toward her, with a bemused expression. A white T-shirt was tossed over his right shoulder, while water beaded and glistened on his bare, muscular chest. She felt herself stir with a deep longing to touch each and every drop with her tongue.

"And they get all the love," she responded, pointing to direct his attention back to the shoreline where the owners were hugging their pet and praising his retrieval skills. "Even when they're all wet."

He smiled, white teeth dazzling in the sun. "Maybe I'll be lucky enough to come back as a dog, in my next life."

His eyes were shielded with dark glasses, so she couldn't see them. It was like they were playing a flirtatious game, and though it was fun, if she didn't hear his answer soon, she would burst.

Liza turned away from the scene on the beach, and slid her sunglasses on top of her head.

"We should all be so lucky. But I don't think you called me down here to talk about dogs."

She leaned her back against the railing, and felt the wood press into her skin like a veiled warning.

"So let's get straight to the point. Have you made a decision?"

Anthony slipped his shirt over his head, and his mood seemed to change along with his clothes. Both of which she was sorry to see happen, but she'd waited over a week to hear the truth.

He wrung the last bit of water from his shorts and straightened the hem of his shirt.

"I have, but I don't think you're going to like what I have to say."

He gestured to a nearby weathered bench, the only one on the pier. "Let's have a seat, and I'll explain."

Liza frowned, a sense of dread welling up inside of her like a cesspool. She willed her feet to move and followed him.

She sat down and when he did the same, she managed to keep her eyes directed to his face, even though she wanted to let them roam down his body.

Anthony held the start of her commercial design career in the palm of his hand, and yet all she wanted to do was check out his package, she thought, chiding herself. But she also knew that a man with a body like his could make any woman forget about priorities.

He turned toward her and draped one elbow on the back of the bench, and she bit the inside of her lip in anticipation of his words.

"Remember when I told you that I was looking at several other architectural firms, in addition to you, to pitch designs for the clinic?"

Liza crossed her legs and her pale yellow skirt, which hit right above the knee, inched up slightly on her left thigh, exposing a little more skin than she'd intended. She left the material where it lay, not wanting to call attention to herself, and was surprised when Anthony's eyes drifted down.

She smiled, enjoying the warmth that slipped through

her veins. Though it was the barest of appraisals, she had to wonder if he liked what he saw.

"Yes. You mentioned that you could not tell me their names. Confidentiality is standard in the industry, so I wasn't concerned."

He swallowed hard. A small lump slid up and down under the skin of his neck.

"I never told you their names, not because of confidentiality, but because they never existed."

Liza uncrossed her legs and sat up straighter.

"What do you mean?"

He looked her directly in the eyes. "I mean that I never requested any other quotes from any other architects, except for you."

"Why, Anthony?" she choked out, as his words filtered through her mind.

He lifted the shades from his eyes, gliding them onto his closely shaved black hair, and folded his arms.

"The answer is simple. I went with my gut. I chose you."

Chose her?

Though Liza knew she should have been happy, the matter-of-fact tone in his voice made her suspicious.

"Just like that?" she asked, moving her hands down to grasp the edge of the bench.

She didn't want any special treatment. She wanted to win, fair and square.

Anthony nodded, his smile cryptic. "More or less."

Her throat felt dry. "But…when? How? I don't understand."

"After the first interview and our first meeting, I

decided to cancel all the other presentations, and take a chance on you. Once I saw your design, I knew I had made the right decision."

He extended his hand. "Congratulations. You got the project!"

She ignored the gesture and stood up, and though she felt as if she were going to faint, she did not wobble.

Something was wrong. Unease trickled through her, like silt settling through pebbles at the bottom of a riverbed. Nothing she'd ever had in her life, that meant something, had come easily.

She stood up and backed away from the bench. "What kind of game are you playing?"

Anthony's hand fell to his side, and a part of her was surprised at the look of shock on his face. She spun on the heels of her sandals and started walking away to the other side of the pier.

She heard his bare feet slap the wood and he jogged to her.

"What are you talking about?"

Liza felt his hand on her shoulder and turned.

"You made me believe that I was competing with other firms for the project, when there really wasn't any competition at all!"

Her voice sounded shrill in her ears. A headache was coming on, joined by the confusion she knew wouldn't go away soon.

"Only with yourself," he said.

The wind blew her hair back, exposing the scar on her jaw.

"Myself? What do you mean?"

Anthony leaned against the wooden railing and nodded.

"When I first met you, you seemed a little unsure, even though you tried to appear confident. I knew that if you thought you were competing with other firms, you would do your very best work."

First, he hides the truth. Now, he's insulting me by acting as if he knows me? Was there no end to the man's arrogance?

She knit her brows together and jerked her thumb against her chest.

"I always do my very best work, no matter what," she insisted angrily, tucking her hair behind her ear.

"Are you sure about that?" Anthony asked, his tone neutral. "Because after our first interview, I did some digging on my own."

At his words, she felt her insides dry up and go hollow. A mix of anger and frustration rolled through her, but she tried to appear unmoved.

"I looked into those commercial deals that you told me fell through, but your explanation checked out okay."

Liza clenched her fists with frustration. "Are you accusing me of lying?"

"Not necessarily. There were other potential commercial deals that you were involved in initially at your former firm. But you weren't showing up at meetings, and when you did, you were distracted and totally not interested in the proceedings."

He paused again. "Ultimately, you were asked to leave. Ring a bell?"

Liza felt her face get hot, and her eyes filled with

angry tears. No way she would lend credence to his words by mentioning that her lackluster performance at her previous job was due to grief.

It was around that time that her mother had passed away suddenly. Shortly after surgery overseas. *Cosmetic* surgery that she didn't really need. Performed by a doctor who claimed he knew what he was doing, and who, in Liza's mind, ultimately had a hand in her untimely death.

Liza swallowed hard, and willed her tears away.

"How dare you investigate me!"

The waves roared in her ears as memories of her mother filtered into her mind, spreading guilt like a bitter balm.

Though she knew she shouldn't be surprised by his inquiries into her life, for some reason, she was hurt.

His voice remained calm. "I go with my gut, but I'm not stupid."

Liza walked a few steps away, blaming her hurt feelings on her deep attraction to him, which was getting stronger, even now, as she fought to regain control of her emotions.

She turned back and put her hands on her hips. "It's all about you, isn't it, Anthony?"

He approached her slowly, and she fought the urge to open her arms and welcome him into hers.

"No. It's all about the clinic."

A smile tugged at the corners of his mouth. "And then, it's all about me."

She glared at him, and uttered an exasperated sigh.

"I'm joking," he said, chuckling lightly. "But, to be

honest, it was important to test your mettle under pressure."

Liza went back to the railing. "Why? I know how to handle myself."

Anthony met her there. "But not in a commercial building situation."

"How long are you going to keep throwing that in my face?"

His bare arm pressed against hers, gently claiming.

Being close to him heightened the swirl of confusing emotions inside her, and she found that her anger was beginning to ebb away.

"Until you believe that I'm giving you the chance of a lifetime."

His brown eyes studied her face, and she felt her cheeks warm under his scrutiny.

She turned her body, leaned her hip against the railing and crossed her arms.

"Not like this, Anthony. I don't know how, and I don't know why, but I feel like you tricked me."

As she was saying those words, he ran his hands down her arms until they fell limply at her sides.

The feel of his hands resonated throughout her body, leaving her with a wave of desire that nearly rocked her off her feet.

"I didn't trick you," he insisted. "I just didn't tell you the whole truth."

He touched the tip of her nose with his finger, and she wanted to melt. The breeze lifted her skirt and caressed her legs, almost tickling her in its gentleness, exciting her in places that were hidden from view.

"And neither did you."

She looked away. Anthony was right. She hadn't told him the whole truth about her mother, and how alone she'd felt losing both of her parents in a short amount of time. And she had no intention of doing so. She had moved to Bay Point to start a new life, and nobody was going to stop her.

"Knowing what you know now, why do you want to work with me?"

"Because you're smart and talented, and I loved your design."

He shrugged, his smile nonchalant. "But if you don't want the project, so be it."

Anthony started moving away again, as if the matter was settled, leaving the decision up to her. The air shifted with him, leaving an invisible void in her heart she couldn't explain.

Liza found herself following him. Suddenly, he turned around and walked back.

He planted his bare feet in front of her sandaled ones, then ran his finger along the underside of her jaw.

She kept her eyes straight ahead and poised on his T-shirt, expectant and not knowing what to expect at the same time.

Suddenly, he lifted her chin as his lips came into view and touched her own. The pressure light and hesitant, asking more than taking, and she felt her lids blink shut.

With her heart pounding in her chest like it was beating for the first time, she succumbed to his kiss. His lips, moist and slightly plump, drew her lips closer at the same time his hands threaded through her hair.

The wind tousled her skirt, and the breeze felt strangely chilly against her thighs. Anthony gently backed up against the railing. She was glad for the support, since her legs felt as loose as a rubber band.

The roaring in her ears was no longer the waves, but an incessant buzz that nothing would be the same between them, no matter if she took the project or not. But in that moment, she didn't care. Nothing mattered but the soft dance of their mouths.

Noses swooping briefly against the apples of their cheeks. Tongues dipping in and out of each other's mouths. Gently stroking and discovering. Rolling forth and crashing through, forever changing the landscape of their relationship.

She cradled her arms around his waist, allowed her hands to travel under his shirt and up his tightly muscled back. Through his swim trunks, she could feel his long, hot flesh throbbing against her abdomen, making her moan as he drew her even closer to him.

Liza was immersed in a sensual pool of desire, the depths unknown, beguiling them both to explore.

A seagull cackled as it landed on the railing near them, and the intrusion forced them apart.

Liza saw that the bird had a small fish in its beak before it took off, wings flapping as hard as she was breathing. She took a step back and could see the heavy bulge, elongated and enticing underneath Anthony's swim trunks, and she longed to feel his flesh upon hers. In hers.

No clothes. No regrets.

He was staring at her, and she looked down, her chest heaving slightly. Her nipples puckered almost painfully inside her lace bra as he traced a finger down the buttons of her white silk blouse.

He ridged his thumb against her lips. Despite the interruption, the air between them was still hot, and warm. Salty with promise, and that, Liza decided right then, was a problem.

She ran her hands over the front of her blouse, hoping to calm herself down, but it had the opposite effect. So she took another two steps back, and watched as he adjusted the waistband of his swim trunks.

"I'll accept the project, Dr. Marbet, with one caveat."

She took a deep breath, still tasting his lips upon hers, his hot breath in her mouth, and hoped she wouldn't regret her words.

"That you never, ever kiss me again."

He slipped a hand under his shirt, exposing his rock solid abs.

"Didn't you like it?"

She tucked her hair behind her ears, and tapped her foot nervously.

"That's a trick question."

She looked away only a moment, and the next thing she knew, Anthony was in front of her again, and it was as if they'd never been apart.

He tilted her chin up with two fingers. "A trick question, with only one answer."

He bent until his lips were hovering over hers. "And that answer is yes."

Liza didn't say a word. She couldn't, as she could barely breathe, let alone speak. Was he going to kiss her again? Oh, but she wanted him to, how desperately she wanted to feel him again.

"But you don't have to say anything," he continued in a low, sexy tone. "Because I can tell that you liked it very much. Your lips are parted right now, waiting for me, and those beautiful eyes of yours are closed like you are in the middle of a dream."

Anthony tilted her chin a little higher, and she opened her eyes, which she hadn't realized were closed. He caressed her cheek, and she reveled in it, because she knew that it wasn't forever.

"But I have no problem keeping this all business. Just as long as you and I agree on one thing—I want you and you want me. That's not going to change. As long as you can handle that, there won't be any problems, and no more kisses."

He let go of her chin and she stared at him, too shocked at his brashness to say anything in return. He started to walk away and she put her hands on her hips.

"Where do you think you're going?"

With the hint of a smile, Anthony turned and drew his T-shirt over his head. He took his time. The slow and sinuous movement allowed her to take his whole body in and commit it to memory.

"For another swim. I feel like I need to cool off."

"FAST FIVE" READER SURVEY

Your participation entitles you to:
✸ 4 Thank-You Gifts Worth Over $20!

Complete the survey in minutes.

Get 2 FREE Books

Your Thank-You Gifts include **2 FREE BOOKS** and **2 MYSTERY GIFTS**. There's no obligation to purchase anything!

See inside for details.

Dear Reader,

Since you are a lover of our books, your opinions are important to us... and so is your time.

That's why we made sure your **"FAST FIVE" READER SURVEY** can be completed in just a few minutes. Your answers to the five questions will help us remain at the forefront of women's fiction.

And, as a thank-you for participating, we'd like to send you **4 FREE THANK-YOU GIFTS!**

Enjoy your gifts with our appreciation,

Pam Powers

To get your
4 FREE THANK-YOU GIFTS:

✳ Quickly complete the "Fast Five" Reader Survey
and return the insert.

◀ **DETACH AND MAIL CARD TODAY!** ▶

"FAST FIVE" READER SURVEY

1 Do you sometimes read a book a second or third time? ○ Yes ○ No

2 Do you often choose reading over other forms of entertainment such as television? ○ Yes ○ No

3 When you were a child, did someone regularly read aloud to you? ○ Yes ○ No

4 Do you sometimes take a book with you when you travel outside the home? ○ Yes ○ No

5 In addition to books, do you regularly read newspapers and magazines? ○ Yes ○ No

YES! I have completed the above Reader Survey. Please send me my 4 FREE GIFTS (gifts worth over $20 retail). I understand that I am under no obligation to buy anything, as explained on the back of this card.

168/368 XDL GJ5L

FIRST NAME	LAST NAME

ADDRESS

APT.#	CITY

STATE/PROV.	ZIP/POSTAL CODE

READER SERVICE—Here's how it works:

Accepting your 2 free Kimani™ Romance books and 2 free gifts (gifts valued at approximately $10.00) places you ur no obligation to buy anything. You may keep the books and gifts and return the shipping statement marked "cancel you do not cancel, about a month later we'll send you 4 additional books and bill you just $5.44 each in the U.S. or $5 each in Canada. That is a savings of at least 16% off the cover price. It's quite a bargain! Shipping and handling is 50¢ per book in the U.S. and 75¢ per book in Canada.* You may cancel at any time, but if you choose to continue, ev month we'll send you 4 more books, which you may either purchase at the discount price or return to us and ca your subscription. *Terms and prices subject to change without notice. Prices do not include applicable taxes. Sales applicable in N.Y. Canadian residents will be charged applicable taxes. Offer not valid in Quebec. Books received may be as shown. All orders subject to approval. Credit or debit balances in a customer's account(s) may be offset by any o outstanding balance owed by or to the customer. Please allow 4 to 6 weeks for delivery. Offer available while quantities l

Chapter 8

The delicious smells emanating from Ruby's Tasty Pastries, Bay Point's most popular gourmet coffee shop and bakery, should have been illegal. Liza couldn't walk within one hundred feet without gaining at least five pounds, or at least it seemed like it.

Every time she left with her stomach full of delicious treats, she felt like she had to run a half marathon. But she always came back for more.

Today was Tuesday, and it was as good a day as any to indulge in her favorite no-no: chocolate croissants. Plus, it was her first official day of working with Anthony, and she needed to be appropriately sugared up for the task.

Liza scored a table next to the open windows. An unexpected bonus, considering the place was packed.

Ruby approached. With her thin figure, short jet-black hair, sienna-colored skin and somewhat pointy ears, she reminded Liza of a '70s television actress.

"I'm going to make you pay for the next scale I break," she joked. "How do you stay so slim?"

"I stick to nibbles and licks," Ruby advised.

She set a plate of pastries Liza had ordered at the counter down in front of her. She picked up one of the croissants, her mouth salivating.

"I don't know how you restrain yourself."

Ruby laughed and removed a steaming cup of café au lait from her tray. "Not my pastries, silly. I was referring to my husband. He's all I need to satisfy my sweet tooth."

Liza giggled. "You're a blessed woman."

Ruby and her husband lived in the apartment above her shop. She'd never met the man, but she heard he was some kind of salesman and that he traveled. A lot. When he got home rumor had it that you could hear the couple's exultant lovemaking sessions all the way down Magnolia Avenue.

When Ruby left, Liza took one bite of her chocolate croissant and moaned with delight.

Food often had a calming kind of effect on her, especially when she was stressed. Since her mother passed, she'd gained a little weight that she'd put off losing for months.

Liza felt safer with a little bit of padding, the slight rounding of her curves that caused some men to stare, others to turn away. But she didn't mind. Her weight protected her from men who, in their hearts, wanted perfection.

She sipped her café au lait, and then took another bite out of her croissant. Today was going to be a good day. The faint smell of salt water, always prevalent in the air, floated into her nostrils, and she thought about the beach, and the last time she saw Anthony.

The contract to design his cosmetic surgery clinic was hers, and with one last passionate kiss, they'd agreed that their relationship was at a stalemate, and would remain that way, as long as they were business partners.

Liza wasn't happy with their mutual decision, and yet, somehow she knew it just had to be this way.

She put her elbow on the table, splayed her fingers on her cheek and rested the curve of her jaw against the palm of her hand, hiding her scar once more.

Despite her physical flaw, Liza was fairly self-confident. She knew she wouldn't appeal to every man, and every man would not interest her. But when a man did find her attractive, she rarely accepted it at face value. She found herself probing his reasoning as the words of her mother swirled in her head.

You're ugly. You'll never find a man.

Liza tossed her hair in attempt to rid her mind of the hateful words, like she had done countless times before. Sometimes it worked.

Her mother, who was a famous model, couldn't stand growing old. Even when Liza was a child, she'd been jealous of her own daughter's youth.

Liza didn't understand, until after her mother died,

how much her mother had suffered through the years from low self-esteem, made worse by the fact that her father worked all the time, putting his career at the hospital ahead of the needs of his wife and daughter.

If her mother were alive today and she knew about her brief encounters with Anthony, she likely would have felt that her mean words were justified. She would have claimed Anthony rejected her because of her scar, or because she wasn't as thin as a stick or any number of ridiculous reasons.

The thought saddened her, and she squeezed her eyes to stop the tears and refocused.

If Liza's fantasies were any indication, her need for Anthony was far from over. She could not let go of the fact that she'd felt more desired by him than by any other man previously, even those she'd trusted enough to love, which weren't many.

Every night since his kiss at the roadhouse and then on the beach, her fingers roamed, trying to release her passion by her own hands.

It wasn't the same, because every morning she awoke, frustrated and physically aching for him.

Though their kisses had been brief, she was dying to know what his lips would feel like elsewhere on her body.

If Anthony could see past his ego and his career into what really mattered, she could potentially fall in love with him, despite their pact to keep their relationship all business.

But could she trust him? That remained to be seen.

"Another café au lait, Liza?"

Roused from her thoughts, she shook her head and smiled.

"It's delicious, Ruby. But if I have more than one, I'll be doing cartwheels down Magnolia Avenue."

"Then how about an emergency visit from your favorite doctor?"

Ruby gasped and stepped back, nearly colliding with Anthony.

She turned around. "Sorry, Dr. Marbet. I heard you, but I didn't see you there."

Dressed in clean scrubs, Anthony moved around her and sat down opposite Liza. He tilted his face up at Ruby, a dazzling smile on his lips.

"You can make it up to me by bringing me a steaming cup of your darkest roast."

Ruby grinned. "You got it!"

When she walked away, Liza folded her hands in her lap and looked around. Folks appeared to be minding their own business, but in Bay Point, one could never be too sure.

She moved her chair in closer to the table and whispered, "Why do you have to be so loud?"

"What do you mean? That's the way I normally talk."

He looked around and lowered his voice. "What's the big deal?"

At that moment, Ruby approached with Anthony's coffee. Liza waited until she was gone before speaking again.

"People might think you're my real doctor."

His voice was almost down to a whisper. "You know I'm not. So, what's the problem?"

She squeezed her hands together, barely hearing his words, as her fears jostled with the sounds of animated conversation and silverware clinking against plates.

"People might think…" Her voice trailed off and she swallowed hard. "People might think I need cosmetic surgery."

"Why would they think that?" Liza arranged her hair with one hand around the curve of her jaw. The gesture was deliberate and involuntary at the same time. One of many ways she attempted to hide her flaw from other people, but she could never hide it from herself.

She saw his eyes flicker downward at her movements, but he didn't seem perturbed, and she recalled when they'd kissed, that he'd caressed her jaw with his fingers.

Suddenly, he reached out, touched her hand and brought it gently back to the table.

She relaxed and felt like he was trying to comfort her as best he could in a public place.

"Who cares what people think. You and I both know you're perfect." With a smile on his lips, he squeezed her hand. "Especially for me."

Her heart skipped a beat at his intimate words. They seemed genuine, but how could she be sure? And did she really want to find out?

The heat of his kiss seared through her mind and she felt a flutter between her thighs. The pleasurable sensation was a reminder to keep their conversations quick, informal and professional. That was the only way she would be able to tamp down, and hopefully cure, her desire for him.

Liza took a sip of coffee. "You shouldn't be holding my hand."

Anthony raised a brow. "Why?"

"The agreement, remember?"

He leaned over and whispered, "That only covered kisses."

His low voice tumbled into her ear, and he nipped her earlobe slightly with his teeth.

She stifled a yelp and looked around, but no one seemed to notice his flirtatious behavior.

Liza hid a smile and moved her chair away before he could get them both into trouble.

"What's gotten into you this morning?" she scolded lightly. "Did you bring the contracts?"

He shook his head. "My attorney emailed them to you. Should be in your inbox this morning."

She dug out her phone from her purse and navigated to her email.

"Don't you trust me?"

Liza found the email and looked up. "It's not a matter of trust. I want to forward it on to my attorney now because he's leaving on vacation tomorrow. Ten days in Tahiti."

"Do you think he'll be able to review it right away?"

"He knows of the urgency, but if he can't, I've known him to respond when he's out of town. He's the type of guy who can't leave it at the office."

"He sounds like me. Neither can I."

Anthony took a sip of his coffee. "This is so strong it would wake the dead."

His body would wake the dead, she thought, noticing how casually sexy he looked in his scrubs. His skin seemed to gleam in the muted light of the shop, appearing supple to the touch. As he set his coffee cup down on the table, his forearm contracted slightly, the muscles sleek and inviting.

Liza averted her eyes down to the menu printed on a paper place mat, and then slowly brought them back to his.

"I'm just curious. What *would* tear you away from the office?" she blurted.

As soon as the words were out of her mouth, she realized he might think she was flirting with him.

And maybe she was. Fact is, she couldn't help herself.

The coffee shop was crowded, and nobody appeared to be listening. Besides, whenever she was around Anthony, she felt as if the world around her disappeared.

"I don't know." He ran a finger around the edge of his cup and shrugged, but his eyes twinkled. "Why don't you suggest something?"

She ventured a small smile. "Let's see. A medical conference? The latest surgical gadget?"

"Nada. You must think I'm a real workaholic."

"Aren't all doctors married to their work? Something about making a difference? Saving the world?"

Anthony leaned back in his chair. "I admit I had dreams of grandeur when I first entered medical school."

"And now?"

He smiled. "I'm satisfied with just changing my patients' lives in my corner of the world, right here in Bay Point."

"Do you feel like you're making a difference?"

He thought a moment. "Yes. If my patients are happy, I'm happy."

"By changing who they are?" she said.

His face contorted a bit, as if he was surprised by her question.

But Liza didn't care. The only thing her mother's cosmetic surgeon cared about was lining his pockets by preying on women with low self-esteem.

She prayed Anthony wasn't the same way, and now was a good time to make sure, before she formally signed a contract to work with him.

He moved his chair closer to hers. "I'm modifying their appearance according to their wishes, that's all."

"By feeding into their negative self-perceptions?"

"Their internal reasoning is really none of my business. My job is to listen to their concerns and set realistic expectations for the outcome."

"So you don't claim to be a miracle worker?"

"No, but my patients think I am. And that's all that counts," he replied, without a trace of the egoism that he often displayed.

His smile was brief, though, and did not reach his eyes. She sensed that he felt insulted.

"But why the interrogation?" he asked. "I feel like I'm on one of those investigative news programs."

She stifled the urge to take his hands in hers, in apology, as she didn't mean to hurt his feelings.

"I'm sorry. I'm just trying to get an understanding of who you are."

He stared at her, a hint of a smile on his face, as he leaned forward. "As a doctor? Or as a man?"

Liza felt her face flush. Both, she wanted to say, but she choked back the word.

She wanted to understand the man, but she didn't want to lose the project, especially since the contract hadn't even been officially signed.

"A doctor, of course," she lied.

She watched his face for any signs of disappointment at her words, but all he did was motion for Ruby.

"Good. But the only thing you have to worry about is designing my clinic, not what goes on within my walls. Are we clear?"

She nodded as Ruby approached the table. Though Liza was glad for the interruption, she stewed quietly at how Anthony's demeanor could change from flirtatious to friendly to stern in the span of a few minutes.

She decided to end the meeting quickly, as graciously as possible, before she said something else to jeopardize their fragile professional relationship.

He requested some mineral water, and when he asked her if she wanted anything else, she declined.

Ruby scribbled the final total and slid the bill upside down on the table.

Anthony rubbed his hands together. "Shouldn't we be talking about next steps? I'm eager to get started."

Liza nodded. "We can. Though it's a bit premature, at this point. The contracts haven't been signed yet."

She refused to smile, determined to show him that she could be just as terse and businesslike as he could be.

He lowered his voice and whispered in her ear. "Does that mean I can kiss you again?"

She felt her heart leap in her chest at the words that so easily trickled out of his mouth and reignited her desire.

It could be a game, and he could simply want her to stroke his ego. She wouldn't fall for it. She didn't want to give him any further indication that she was interested in him as more than just another rung in the stepladder of her career.

"Only if you want me to scream," she whispered back.

Ignoring the shocked look on his face, she dug out a few bills and placed them on the table.

Anthony touched her wrist gently. "Hey. I was teasing. Let me get that, okay?"

She shouldered her purse, shook her head and grabbed the check from the table.

"No worries, I'll write it off. See you later."

Before he could say another word, she walked away. She resisted the urge to look back and see if he was following her, but there was no need. She felt his eyes boring a hole into her back and her face burned in response.

Ruby normally kept the door open in the mornings, when the weather was cooler. When Liza reached it, she heard a squeal of delight.

"Liza! I'm so glad to see you! Are you still coming to our meeting this afternoon?"

Mrs. Harrill was a tall, extremely thin woman with the booming voice of a sports announcer.

"Yes, I planned on it."

She clapped her hands together, as if she'd just heard the best news of her life.

"Wonderful! The members of our historical society will be so pleased!" she exclaimed.

Liza resisted the urge to put her hands over her ears. "I'm looking forward to it," she replied with a polite smile.

Mrs. Harrill had her body angled in such a way that she would have knocked the woman over if she'd tried to go outside.

So she couldn't budge.

"Oh, hello. Dr. Marbet. I didn't see you there."

Liza swiveled around. "That happens a lot," she muttered to herself as her elbow brushed against Anthony's abdomen. When she felt his hand on her shoulder, she thought she would melt right onto the floor.

"Mrs. Harrill. You're looking well."

"You would know, Dr. Marbet," she said, beaming, and Liza wondered what she was implying.

He gestured toward the door. "We were actually just leaving."

Mrs. Harrill's brows pinched together and she stared at them as if they'd committed some crime. "We?" she asked, her voice lowered. "Well, don't let me keep you both."

"Thank you," Anthony replied, gently steering Liza forward.

Mrs. Harrill left the doorway and entered the coffee shop, so they could pass through freely.

"Liza, we can't wait to hear about your plans to help us restore the old schoolhouse," she turned and called.

Anthony grabbed Liza's hand, and pulled her away.

Some of the people who were sitting on the patio lifted their heads. Since she was so new in town, she didn't recognize any of them, but she bet they knew Anthony.

He held on to her hand tightly, until they were around the corner, then he abruptly let go. When he did, Liza felt a strange sense of abandonment that made her suddenly angry.

She put her purse back on her shoulder, from where it had slipped to her wrist.

"What was that about?" she asked, somehow managing to keep her voice level.

"Remember how I told you that Maisie was always trying to hook me up with someone."

Liza nodded. In addition to being a highly sought-after cosmetic surgeon, he was also known around town for his refusal to date local women, so he was always fodder for a good rumor.

"Mrs. Harrill is her partner in crime. I think they have some kind of bet on who will introduce me to the woman who will be my wife."

Liza's cheeks burned. The man flirting with her again, but this time, she was in no mood to reciprocate, or encourage him.

"Well, it certainly won't be me," she retorted.

If Anthony couldn't keep up his half of their agreement, she'd have to do it for him, she thought as she walked away.

But in her heart, she longed to run back into his arms.

Chapter 9

Liza fluffed her hair in front of her ears and stepped out of her truck. She blinked, her eyes adjusting to the early-morning sun. It was warm so she'd worn a pair of denim shorts and a T-shirt. Today, she and Anthony were meeting with the man she was recommending to lead the construction of the clinic.

She leaned against her vehicle and sighed. She hadn't spoken to Anthony since she'd walked off and left him on Magnolia Avenue. They'd only communicated via email and their lawyers.

She missed his smile, though she often didn't know what was behind it. She missed his body, though she'd never really touched it. But most of all, she missed him.

She bent to tighten the laces on her new steel-toe boots. They were months away from beginning construction, but she had bought a pair anyway. She planned on using the time to break them in, before they broke ground on the clinic.

Out of the corner of her eye, Liza saw Anthony's truck approach.

She heard the car door slam and his shoes crunching on gravel, but she kept her head down as he rushed to her side.

"Are you okay? Another problem with your ankle?"

Liza focused on her laces, as his words swept over her like a gentle wave.

He sounded as if he was concerned about her, as if he cared. But was that just because he was a doctor and had taken an oath to assist anyone who appeared to be in need? Or was it because he had feelings for her?

He knelt down in front of her and lifted her chin to face him.

"Liza, are you okay?"

Her eyes met his and it was like a billion stars exploded between them, so intense was the heat. It was instantaneous, undeniable and incredibly hot.

This time, there was no denying the attraction between them, and her need for him. It would be like denying her need for food and water. There was no doubt he cared about her, but there was nothing she could do about it.

They'd made a promise, and she had to be strong for both of them.

Liza stood up and put her hands on her hips. "Yes. Can't I tie my own shoe laces without you coming to my rescue?"

He rose slowly, and she could see the hurt in his eyes.

Inwardly, she chastised herself for sounding so irritable, when all she wanted to do was throw her arms around his neck so hard that they'd both fall to the ground. He'd kiss her and neither of them would care about the gravel digging into their skin, because the pleasure would outweigh the pain.

But that was a five-second fantasy. In real life, the pain always outlasted the pleasure. Anthony was a gorgeous risk, best to keep him safely in her mind and out of her bed.

"Sorry, I was just trying to help."

She leaned back against the truck. "And I was only teasing."

Anthony shoved his hands in his jeans, and braced his hip against his own vehicle. He seemed wary of her now, and that saddened her.

"Thanks for setting up this meeting so early." He glanced down at his watch, and back up at her. "I've got about an hour before I have to be at the hospital."

She turned away from his eyes and pulled her phone out of her back pocket. "Trent should be here any minute."

"Good guy?"

She nodded. "The best. I've used him on a couple of other projects, not here of course, but in other parts of Northern California."

They fell into an uneasy silence. Their trucks were parked close to each other. If she stretched out her arms, she could have touched him.

She hadn't worn her sunglasses this morning, and

neither had he. They were naked to each other in that respect, and could not hide behind them.

Anthony made no secret of his desire for her. It was as palpable in the air between them as the scent of the ocean.

She saw his eyes caress her body, travel down her legs and back up again to her face.

His actions didn't make her feel uncomfortable; instead, they set off tiny fireworks of yearning that made her quiver inside. She wanted to do the same thing to him, but with her mouth. If he could see what was going through her mind, he might have had a heart attack from shock.

Anthony cleared his throat and she jumped a little. He walked to the front of his truck and stopped.

"The place hasn't changed much," he said, turning back.

Her voice caught in her throat at the hint of a smile on his lips. His low tone seemed to glide through the air and wrap around her, comforting in its sexiness.

Liza squinted, even though the sun, at seven o'clock in the morning, wasn't very bright yet.

"Yes, it's still a broken-down motel," she said, wryly. *And I still think I might be falling in love with you.*

She took in a sharp breath at her thought. Denying her feelings for Anthony was easy. Admitting them to herself was not.

In two steps, he was at her side, and for a moment, she panicked, thinking she had actually voiced that she was in love with him, rather than simply thought the words. It was early, she hadn't had any coffee and so her mind was a little groggy. Plus, she was anxious about seeing him again. Anything could happen.

He put his elbow on the hood of her truck, near the front windshield. "How are you, really?"

"I'm fine, Anthony," she said, without looking at him. If she did, she knew she would drown in his eyes. "Just anxious to get started."

"I know. Me, too."

His voice was so close; his body even closer. She felt her legs wobble, and dug the heels of her boots deeper into the gravel to stabilize them. But there was nothing she could do to calm the rapid beating of her heart.

She checked her phone again. *Where was Trent?*

Anthony reached for her, and she turned around and faced him.

The tug of his hand caused a chain reaction and she felt the pull of his body, like some kind of sensual magnet. Her breasts felt heavier than usual, nipples tightening.

But rather than close the gap between them, though she desperately wanted to, she kept her hip firmly against the warm metal of her truck. As if the vehicle could protect her from the desire that was swiftly threatening to overtake her.

"I'm sorry about the other day. Back at Ruby's. I didn't mean to upset you. When you walked away without saying goodbye, I realized I did."

She couldn't believe he was actually apologizing. His words sounded so sincere, causing her eyes to smart with tears. She blinked away the moisture, glad for the slight breeze in the air.

His palm was cool to the touch, but her hand jerked a little as if she'd been burned. Still, he didn't let go, and Liza didn't pull away. She remained where she was, her hand in his, her body leaning against the truck, her right arm pressed against the glass.

Silence fell between them, the sounds of birds filling the space where their mutual desire was inescapable.

"Don't worry about it," she managed to say, trying on an impersonal, professional tone. Her voice sounded thin and narrow in her ears, not full and lush like his.

"Now that the deal is settled and the contract is signed, there's a lot to do."

His eyes drifted down to her lips and lit a fire there, too. She licked them involuntarily, remembering the passion that his kisses had invoked weeks ago. Since that time, her need for him had never gone away. It had only grown stronger.

"Lots to keep us busy," he said, his breath a bit ragged.

Her lips parted in anticipation, and she dropped her eyes from his, realizing he was watching her intently.

She stared at her boots, as if they were the most interesting things in the world, trying to think of what to say next, something that wouldn't give her thoughts or feelings away.

He drew his knuckles down lightly across her jaw. She lifted her eyes, and what she saw in his, nearly rocked her off her feet.

"Liza, I—"

His words were cut off by the loud roar of a motorcycle approaching. She jumped and Anthony dropped his hand to his side. She pressed her back against her vehicle, heart pounding, just as Trent rode up and parked on the other side.

Had he seen Anthony touching her? It was hard to tell because Trent was wearing a helmet, with the dark shield pulled down to protect his eyes.

The feel of Anthony's skin upon hers lingered as she walked around her truck to greet him.

"Hey, glad you could make it out this morning," she said, wiping her palms on her shorts.

Trent got off his midnight blue motorcycle and slowly took his helmet off. Standing well over six feet tall, he was dressed in jeans, dirty work boots and a blood-red T-shirt. His tattooed arms were hard and muscular, with hands so large they looked like they could take out three men with one punch.

Though Trent appeared, and sometimes acted, like a rebel, she knew he was just a teddy bear at heart.

She was sure that with his dark skin, warm brown eyes and his rough-and-ready aura, he had plenty of women who would hop on his motorcycle with him and ride away into the sunset.

She wasn't one of them.

Liza waited for Anthony to join her before making introductions.

"Trent Waterson. Meet Dr. Anthony Marbet, the owner of the property."

"Just call me Anthony. I'm looking forward to working with you."

Trent tucked his helmet under one heavily muscled bicep, and the two men shook hands.

"Pleasure."

He stepped back and took a rag from the back of his jeans. As he wiped the sweat away from his close-cropped hair, he let out a slow whistle.

"Looks like the motel has seen better days, but I'm guessing a whole lot of hot lovin' was made between these walls."

Liza felt her cheeks warm and saw the corners of Anthony's mouth tilt up when he caught her watching his reaction. She guessed he wasn't uncomfortable at all at Trent's comment.

He gestured toward the old motel and nodded in agreement. "Time to bury her."

"Trent loves demolishing buildings, isn't that right?"

Trent stuck the rag back in his pocket and set his helmet on the seat of his motorcycle.

"Damn straight," he grunted and made a fist. "Destroying things is my favorite part of the construction process."

Liza grinned. "Boys will be boys, won't they? Let me give you a tour before you run off and get your dozer."

The two men started to walk away.

"Wait!" she exclaimed. "I brought my tablet with the design renderings so you can get a better sense of the scope of this project."

"Sounds good," Trent said distractedly as his phone started to ring. He unclipped it from his belt and glanced at the screen.

"Do you mind if I take this call?"

Liza shook her head. "Take your time."

She watched as Trent walked some distance away in

the opposite direction for what was obviously a very private call. Then, she leaned into the open window of her truck, but she couldn't quite reach the device.

"Need some help?"

Liza turned around quickly. Just the sound of Anthony's voice made her weak in the knees, and she savored the pleasure he unknowingly caused, glad they were alone, where Trent couldn't see them.

"Y-yes," she stuttered. "I can't reach it."

"I'll get it. I have long arms," he said, in a low, sexy tone.

Liza had plenty of room to step back, a foot or two, a yard or twenty, to give him extra space. But she stayed exactly where she was, rooted in desire that she couldn't explain, but wanted to continue to dwell in.

She wanted him to touch her.

Anthony maneuvered his body between the passenger-side mirror and her. As he reached into her truck, his arm grazed slowly against her breasts, and underneath her thin T-shirt, her nipples hardened instantly. She knew he could probably feel them, and if he could feel them, she knew he'd want to touch them again.

His abdomen leaned against the metal of her truck. She pressed her hand against his back, and could feel his muscles tense and move. He didn't shrink away, and neither did she, until he emerged from the open window.

He handed her the tablet, his eyes on her lips, as if tasting them again in his mind, like she had done so many times since their first kiss.

Suddenly he traced his finger along her jaw, to the

middle of her chin, down her neck and over her right breast, making a tiny, swift circle around her nipple.

A breathless moan escaped from her lips, and she clamped one hand over her mouth at the sound of Trent's footsteps on the gravel.

Liza blushed, clutched the tablet in her arms and stepped back just as Trent reached the two vehicles.

Though he'd unknowingly interrupted a private moment, she was glad that he did. Being alone with Anthony, even for a moment, always made her feel like she was on the edge of losing control.

"Sorry about that folks," said Trent.

Liza cleared her throat. "No problem."

Anthony led them through the archway to the back of the property. "Let me show you around while Liza powers up her device, although I suspect it might be warm enough already."

The two men strode away, but Anthony looked back briefly, a devious smile on his face, and she felt her cheeks heat up again.

At the sight of the Pacific Ocean, Trent hooked his thumbs into the belt loops of his jeans, and whistled low. "I wish I'd rode here in my dozer instead of my motorcycle. I'd tear this whole place down right now, just for that view right there."

"I told you it was fabulous, didn't I?" Liza said, hugging her tablet to her chest.

"There really are no words," Anthony commented. "And with Liza's design, my clinic will be just as beautiful."

Her insides warmed at his compliment, and she swiped across the screen of her tablet.

"Here, Trent," she said, navigating to the app that held all her blueprints. "Let me show you."

Thirty minutes later, the trio was back in front of the motel, and the two men were shaking hands goodbye.

"I assume Liza has already informed you of our construction budget?"

Trent nodded. "It'll be tight, but I'll make it work. I've lived in Bay Point for a while and have built up a tight crew of local guys. We'll get it done."

"Looking forward to getting that contract, Liza."

She smiled. "It will be in your inbox this evening."

"Terrific. The sooner my men and I can start pounding this old motel back into dust, the better."

Trent turned away and put on his motorcycle helmet, and then a pair of black leather gloves she hadn't seen before.

As much as she wanted to, Liza didn't dare stick around and wait until Trent was gone so that she could be alone with Anthony.

After waving goodbye, she got into her truck and carefully set the tablet onto the passenger seat. She put the key into the ignition, turned it and nothing happened. She tried multiple times and…nothing.

Anthony came up to her open window on the driver's side, while Trent stuck his head in the open window on the passenger side.

"Want me to try?" Anthony asked.

"And if the doc can't do it, let me have a go."

She nodded and got out of the truck, and handed her keys to Anthony. But after several tries, it wouldn't start for him either.

"It might be a dead battery," he said and got out of the truck, a grim look on his face.

"If that's the case," Trent said, "then my magic fingers won't work either."

Liza lightly smacked her forehead with the heel of her palm. "It probably is. I saw an indicator light on the dashboard last week, but I didn't pay any attention to it."

Anthony handed her keys back to her. "I'd give you a jump but I have to be at the hospital soon."

"I can take you home, Liza," Trent offered. "Then you could call a tow truck and have them bring it back to the service station."

Liza breathed a sigh of relief. "Can you, Trent? I'd appreciate it, though I don't want to be any trouble."

"It's no trouble at all, just as long as you don't mind hopping on the back of my cycle and wearing my helmet."

He walked away as if the matter was settled.

Liza's truck was so old that she had to manually roll up the windows. Once that was done, she locked the passenger door from the inside, grabbed her tablet and got back out. She was locking the driver's side door when Anthony came up to her.

"Change of plans. I'll take Liza home," he announced. His authoritative tone seemed to dare anyone to challenge him.

Liza's heart began to pound again, with more excitement than uncertainty. Wasn't this what she really wanted? To be alone with Anthony?

Trent tucked his helmet under his arm. "Are you sure? I thought you had to be at the hospital."

Anthony nodded, and opened the passenger door of his truck, as if Liza was immediately supposed to get in. She did anyway, just to avoid an argument.

"It's okay. I'll have someone cover for me until I get there."

Liza put her tablet on the spotless floor mat, and waved goodbye to Trent, who shrugged, strapped on his helmet and rode away.

Anthony got in, started the ignition and draped his hand across the front seat as he backed out.

A few minutes later, he pulled onto the entrance ramp of Highway 101 and eased into the flow of traffic.

"When can we break ground?"

She settled back in her seat. "It's going to be a few months, Anthony. I'll know more soon. Luckily, Trent knows his way around the sea of permits we're going to have to get before we even bulldoze the place."

"Remember, I'm hoping the project will be completed in eighteen months or less."

She nodded. "I know. It's an aggressive timeline, but I'll do everything in my power to meet it."

When he pulled up in front of the bed-and-breakfast, Liza was sorry she had to leave.

"You didn't have to give me a ride, Anthony."

He glanced over at her. "Trent is a nice guy. But motorcycles are dangerous," he replied, flipping on the air-conditioning.

She raised a brow. "Oh, is that all? You're just concerned about my safety?"

"No, I'd just rather have your arms around my waist than his."

"A little jealous?" she teased.

"That depends," Anthony said, tapping his thumbs against the steering wheel. "Has he kissed you?"

"No!" she answered, appalled. "I don't go around kissing contractors."

"But you do kiss cosmetic surgeons, hmm?"

"Only when they kiss me first."

His lips brushed softly against hers, and though Liza wanted to return his kiss more than anything, she pushed him away gently.

"Stop. What about our agreement?"

"A man can change his mind, can't he?" He leaned over, and stroked the back of her neck. "Now I've just got to change yours."

Liza touched the tip of her finger to his mouth.

They were two people in lust, and one person falling in love, she thought.

"It'll be fun trying," she said, with a coy smile.

Before he could kiss her again, she picked up her tablet and hopped out of the truck.

Chapter 10

Liza looped her arm through Maisie's and helped her down the stairs of the bed-and-breakfast.

"You sure you don't mind walking with me?" Maisie asked, holding on to the railing.

They were on their way to a ribbon-cutting ceremony to celebrate the official opening of the new Bay Point City Hall.

"Don't be silly, Maisie. We're going to the same event. Why shouldn't we go together?"

"Because I know a young man who would be a much more good-looking escort."

Liza waited until they had reached the redbrick pathway before speaking again.

"If you're talking about Dr. Marbet, might I remind you that he and I are business partners only?"

Maisie tugged on her arm. "Oh, so what about those flowers he sent you this week?"

The arrival of the bouquet, a mix of red roses, white daisies, baby's breath and eucalyptus, had brought a smile to Liza's face and a lot of confusion to her mind.

She'd placed them on the bureau in her room. The fragrance filled the small space, and reminded her of him every night when she fell asleep. There was no note, only his signature on the florist's card.

"Congratulatory only," Liza interjected. "In celebration of our partnership."

"Wait a minute. He's your client. So shouldn't you be the one sending him the flowers?"

They stepped out onto the sidewalk, turned left and headed down Magnolia Avenue. They passed a variety of shops, including Blooms in Paradise and an antique store that she loved to browse.

Maisie was right. Since she was now self-employed, there were no stupid corporate rules that said she couldn't send a token of appreciation to a new client.

But Anthony was different. He was a client, yet in her heart, he was so much more.

All week, she'd thought about going to the shop and asking Vanessa if Anthony had purchased them himself, or if he'd had one of the hospital's administrative assistants do it. If he picked out the types of flowers, or if Vanessa had taken care of that, but she never worked up the nerve.

In a town like Bay Point, asking too many questions could land her smack in the middle of the rumor mill, if she wasn't churning there already.

"Dr. Marbet's going to have most of my time for the next eighteen to twenty-four months as his clinic is being built. Trust me, he doesn't need any flowers."

Maisie stopped and adjusted her bright pink hat over her frosted gray hair. The unique color combination brought out the beauty of her nut-brown skin.

"No, what he needs is a wife," she exclaimed, as if that little fact had just settled in her mind.

Liza shook her head in disbelief. This was the second time the subject of matrimony had come up in the past few weeks.

"I don't think marriage is for me. It's too...permanent."

"Mark my words, Liza. You'll change your tune when you meet the right man," Maisie predicted. "In fact, maybe you already have!"

Even in the twilight, Liza could see the old woman's eyes sparkling.

"Now hold on to my arm tight," Maisie instructed, as they headed toward the entrance graced by yellow and blue balloons. Liza was surprised to see a large crowd already gathered inside the rotunda, where the main festivities were being held.

The Bay Point High School jazz band serenaded the attendees with a fairly decent rendition of Miles Davis's "Kind of Blue."

Mayor Langston approached, dressed in a tuxedo, his lovely and very pregnant wife, Vanessa, at his side. With their arms around each other's waists, they both looked very happy, and according to rumor, it was not a public facade. Their love was as real and as true as it got, despite the pressure of being in the local political and social spotlight.

"Hello, ladies, I'm so glad you're both here."

Maisie touched the tip of her hat. "I wouldn't have missed this event for the world, Mayor. Besides," she said with a conspiratorial grin, "I've got DVR so I won't miss any of my Saturday night shows."

He laughed. "And Liza, when I heard you'd gotten the contract with Dr. Marbet, I was really pleased. Your design was outstanding."

Liza smiled and shook his hand. "Thank you, Mayor. I worked hard on it. This project is really important to me."

And so was the man who hired her.

She looked around to see if she could spot Anthony, but he was nowhere to be seen.

Maybe he'd gotten caught up at the hospital.

"Liza, would you excuse me?" said the mayor, his tone urgent. "I'd like to talk to Maisie privately for a moment."

"No problem," she said.

"I'll be right back, honey," Mayor Langston said to his wife, before turning and leading Maisie away.

"I wonder what that's about," Liza said to Vanessa.

"Just a last-ditch effort to convince Maisie to cut the official ribbon."

"That's odd. She usually wants to be the center of attention. She doesn't want to do it?"

"Apparently not." Vanessa smiled, and added, "But my husband can be very convincing when he wants to be."

Liza grinned and extended her hand. "I don't think we've formally met. I'm Liza Sinclair. I've only been in Bay Point a few months, but I know you own the flower shop in town."

Vanessa nodded. "Pleased to meet you. I've known Maisie for years. She's such a doll."

"Can I ask you a question?"

"Sure, what is it?"

Liza gripped her white clutch purse tightly. "I received a bouquet of flowers from your shop, from Dr. Marbet. Did he place the order by phone or did he come in?"

Vanessa's smile widened. "Not only did he come in, but he personally picked out every flower in that arrangement. Wanted each one to be perfect. It took him about thirty minutes."

Liza's heart thudded hard as realization dawned. "I can hardly believe it."

"I know, I couldn't either, because let me tell you that it is so rare for someone to do that, especially a man."

Vanessa sighed and ran her hands over her baby bump. "The man definitely has good taste. It was very obvious that he cares about you and wanted you to like the arrangement."

"I loved it," she admitted, but a pang of guilt struck her insides as she said the words.

She'd thanked him via text, when he'd really deserved a phone call. But just hearing his voice set off pangs of longing deep in her belly, and after the kiss he'd given her in his truck, she'd tried to avoid personal contact.

Since the meeting with Trent, she'd been communicating with Anthony primarily via email and text to negotiate the construction contract and timing.

In hindsight, not calling him, especially after all the time and trouble he'd taken to select the perfect flowers for her, was downright rude.

Vanessa cleared her throat, interrupting Liza's thoughts.

"If you'll excuse me, my husband is motioning for me to join him at the podium."

Liza tilted her head toward Vanessa. "If you could keep what we discussed just between you and me, I would appreciate it."

Vanessa raised her brows. "No problem," she said, nodding in agreement before walking away.

Liza wove her way through the crowd to the refreshment table. She had no doubt in her mind that Vanessa would keep her inquiry a secret.

She ignored the cookies and pastries table, even though they were donated by Ruby, and poured herself a cup of fruit punch. Then she faded into the back of the rotunda near where she and Maisie had entered, to people-watch.

There were lots of animated and energetic conversations going on, and everyone seemed to know one another.

Liza knew that if she was going to make Bay Point her permanent home, she was going to have to come out of her shell and talk to people.

She was never very good at that, but perhaps it was time for a change.

She was on her way back to the refreshment table, but stopped dead in her tracks halfway there.

Anthony, and on his arm, a very blonde and very beautiful Eloise Bradshaw, were standing with their backs to the punch bowl, heads nearly touching, engaging in what looked to be a very private conversation.

Eloise had on a strapless, bright yellow maxi dress that even from a short distance Liza could tell accentuated her large breasts.

Perhaps it was the way Eloise had her arm looped through Anthony's, in a way claiming him for her own. In Liza's mind, they looked very much like a couple, and she had two choices: ignore it or accept it.

Although she knew that appearances could be deceiving, validating that Eloise and Anthony were anything more than friends or business partners was too risky for her heart.

She wouldn't know what to do if the answer was "yes."

Liza turned away from the scene and searched the crowd for someone she knew. After a few moments, she found Mrs. Harrill near the front of the rotunda. She was just about to set off to further discuss her thoughts on renovating the old schoolhouse, when she heard Anthony's voice calling her name.

Liza didn't look back and ignored him, assuming Eloise was still latched to his side. She kept moving through the crowd, until she felt a tap on her shoulder.

She turned around and kept her face neutral, even as a range of emotions tangled up inside of her.

Anger that he and Eloise looked a little too cozy.

Shame that she had been too fearful of the truth to confront them.

Lust as her eyes quickly took in his navy suit, crisp white shirt and yellow tie. To match Eloise's yellow gown, she thought miserably.

"Hey, didn't you hear me calling you?"

"No," she lied. "It's awfully loud in here."

At her words, he took her by the elbow and led her to a small area where there were chairs set up. Many elderly Bay Point residents were there, and a couple of the men were playing an impromptu card game as they waited for the ribbon cutting to begin.

"Besides," she continued, "it looked like you and Eloise were busy."

Anthony leaned against a round support column and gave her a questioning look. He drew her closer to him, but then dropped her hand, as if it was hot to the touch.

Or maybe he was too embarrassed to hold it in public, she surmised. She could respect that, *if* he hadn't allowed Eloise to hang all over him like wet laundry on a clothesline.

"Liza, it may be loud in here, but I distinctly heard a note of jealousy in your voice."

He'd sounded pleased as he whispered the words in her ear, sending tingles down her spine.

Though she was grateful that he hadn't shouted them to the whole room, he had no right to insinuate she was jealous, even though his assessment was spot-on.

"I'm not jealous," she insisted, keeping her voice low to ensure the old-timers, or anybody else within distance, couldn't hear.

"But she was acting like she was your girlfriend, rather than simply your investor."

"And what do you think you're acting like?"

His voice teased, but also brought her speeding back to reality.

What had she been thinking? She had no right to claim him, just as he had no right to claim her. They were business partners who were madly attracted to each other and who probably always would be.

"You're right, Anthony. Your relationship with Eloise is none of my business."

He crossed his arms over his chest. "There is no relationship. But even if there was, you're too beautiful to be jealous."

His eyes traced the curves of her body, clad in a tea-length ivory silk dress with a sweetheart neckline.

But before Liza could respond, Eloise sidled up to Anthony's side.

"There you are," she cooed. "I've been looking all over for you. The ceremony is about to start soon and Mayor Langston wants us up on stage."

She didn't seem to notice Liza at all, but kept her eyes peeled on Anthony's lips. Probably because he doesn't have his wallet out, Liza thought wryly.

She cleared her throat and Eloise turned with a look of surprise.

"Miss Sinclair. I didn't see you there."

"It's okay. I can see you were otherwise occupied."

At her words, Eloise stepped away from Anthony, as if she'd just realized what a spectacle she'd been making of herself.

"We're so excited that you're going to design the clinic, aren't we, Anthony?"

He nodded and kept his eyes on hers, his slight smile mischievous. "I knew she was the one, the whole time."

His words seemed meant just for her, and her stomach did the kind of flip-flop that would likely stay with her throughout the evening.

"Can I have everyone's attention, please?"

A female voice that Liza recognized as Vanessa's rang through the rotunda.

"If everyone could make their way forward, we're about to start the ceremony."

"Come on, Anthony," Eloise said, reaching for his hand.

He stepped back, just out of reach. "I prefer to watch from here. I'm expecting a call from the hospital and if I'm with everyone at the podium, I'll disturb the ceremony when I have to leave."

Eloise narrowed her eyes, and then shrugged and hurried away. Everyone started to move to the front of the rotunda. Even the old-timers stopped playing cards and shuffled slowly away.

Liza started to follow them, but Anthony caught her wrist from behind and stopped her.

She looked toward the front of the rotunda, where Mayor Langston was already at the podium thanking everyone for attending. Maisie had an outlandishly large pair of blue scissors in her hand, ready to cut the yellow satin ribbon stretched between two support columns.

"Let's get out of here," Anthony whispered, tugging her hand.

Leave the ceremony? For what reason and what could he possibly want?

Her thoughts raced with the possibilities, none of them good. When her mother had died, she'd left her with a legacy of negative thinking. It was something that Liza struggled with on a daily basis.

She bit her lip, not sure if she should go with him.

Maybe he was going to tell her the truth about his availability for a relationship. Though he said he and Eloise weren't an item, that didn't mean some other lucky lady wasn't.

Whenever she met someone nice, she never gave the relationship a chance to flourish. She was always the one to end it, before her own heart got broken. Her mother's damaging words—that she would never have a good man—had become a self-fulfilling prophecy.

She shook her head. "I came here with Maisie. How will she get home?"

"I'm sure Prentice will take her," he replied, tugging her away. "Once she wakes him up from his post where he's *supposed* to be providing security."

Liza masked a giggle.

"Okay, if you think we don't need to be here."

"What I want to do is far more important."

The determination in his voice gave her a little thrill. She allowed him to take her hand and lead her away, curious what he had in mind.

They snuck past the dozing Prentice and out the front door of City Hall. The carousel was ablaze in lights, waiting for riders, but Anthony didn't seem to notice.

She thought he would drop her hand when they got

outside, but he didn't. He held on tight, and she didn't mind at all.

"I need some private time with you. Let's go to your place," he muttered.

Liza silently agreed, since there were no guests at the bed-and-breakfast, and Maisie was out for the night.

A few minutes later, they reached Maisie's darkened front porch and climbed the steps. She gestured to a bench, but Anthony shook his head.

The only illumination was the orangey glow from a nearby old-fashioned streetlight. Hidden by rose bushes and shrubbery, the couple had complete privacy.

He slipped his hands around her waist and she shivered at his touch.

"What's this about, Anthony?"

"I'm trying to decide whether I should kiss you for the last time."

Her mouth watered at the thought of his lips on hers again. She'd barely had a taste of him and now he was talking about "the last time"? Life was so unfair.

"What do you mean?"

"I'm really crazy about you, and it's getting more difficult to maintain control, especially now that the contracts are signed and we're ready to begin work on the clinic."

"It's a two-year job," she reminded him.

"I know. And that's the problem."

Anthony nuzzled his nose against her hair and tightened his grip on her waist. "I don't know if I can work with you for that long and not get deeply involved with you."

She stared at his yellow tie, not quite ready to look at him, afraid that even in the dim light, he would see the desire in her eyes.

He pulled her to him tightly, and she could feel the strength of his erection. She leaned her forehead against his chest and smiled, wanting to dance with happiness at the physical proof that he wanted her, too.

On impulse, Liza drew her finger down the front of his pants, and she resisted the urge to unzip them, discovering that his penis was as hard as steel.

"Is this your way of changing my mind?" she asked.

He sucked in a breath, and then groaned as she scratched the fabric lightly. He grabbed her hand and stopped her.

"One of them."

Liza put both hands on his cheeks and looked into his eyes.

"It's working," she whispered.

She looped her arms around his neck and without another word, Anthony swept his lips lightly across hers before hungrily devouring them.

Plentiful with passion, rich with longing, their lips moved together and he collapsed hard against her, wedging her against the front door.

Liza felt his hand leave her waist and travel up between their bodies and claim her left breast. His thumb gently flicked the hardened tip of her nipple, as his tongue swept against her upper lip.

The initial, gentle probing soon ventured deeper, and he explored the inside of her mouth. With a deep moan she didn't care if anybody heard, she pulled his head down hard against her lips, wanting more, needing more.

After a long while, Liza nudged him away with her shoulder and met his eyes. "Let's go inside."

He nodded and she got her keys out of her purse. On their way upstairs to her room, he placed his hands on her buttocks, stopping her.

"Are you sure there's no one here?" he whispered.

She turned around, and held back a trembling sigh at his touch. "The place is empty this weekend. Don't you trust me?"

"I don't know. That smile you're giving me seems mighty devious."

She grinned and wiggled her ass in response.

When they reached the second landing, Anthony swooped her up in his arms. She laughed and held on tight, planting soft kisses on his neck during the final flight up.

After opening the door with one hand, he took her straight to her bed. The only light was the soft glow of a little lamp, sitting on top of her bureau. It was a habit of hers to leave it on when she went out at night, as she hated to return to a dark room.

He lay down on top of her, loosened his tie and looked into her eyes.

"Are you sure?"

Liza nodded, as she undid his belt buckle and reached for him. His large penis sprung forth, and she moistened at the sight of him, delighted that he was as ready for her as she was for him.

"I want this... I want you more than anything."

She stroked him slowly and gently, while he hurriedly undressed.

Finally, he was naked, and he was as perfect as she'd imagined—toned and muscular and tight in all the right places.

Anthony unzipped her dress and drew it down over her shoulders. He took his time, and didn't rush.

"You're beautiful," he muttered thickly, and her skin prickled at the need in his voice.

He took her hand in his, and flattened her palm and pressed it between her legs.

"Do you feel how wet you are?"

She nodded, and then moaned as he guided her hand against her underwear, now soaked through with moisture.

"Show me," he commanded, his voice a low growl.

He was making her pleasure herself, making her need him even more.

She bit her lips as he lay down next to her, watching her body writhe. Her other hand groped for him desperately, but he wouldn't let her touch him.

"Oh baby, that's good. Too good," he coaxed as he pushed her legs open and knelt before her. "You need a break."

She craned her head up, as he took off her underwear and replaced her hand with his tongue. It darted along her flesh, cresting and teasing, making her whimper.

Liza melted back onto the pillow. She clutched and pawed at his head, as he explored deeper and deeper, until she felt she'd go mad, until she was just about to go over the edge.

Anthony straddled her then, seeming to sense that she was about to come, and she clasped his buttocks with her hands, drawing him toward her mouth, wanting so badly to taste him, too.

"No," he said, and then brought his mouth to hers.

Tasting herself in his mouth was so sensual. Their tongues were like individual flames, burning hotter with every kiss, every lick.

She laced her hands around the back of his head, as his tongue traveled lower to her neck, and nibbled in that place that always made her laugh.

He cupped her breasts, thumbing her nipples until they were button stiff.

His eyes met hers, and she saw they were glazed over with desire.

"So luscious," he said and oh, how she moaned when he finally sucked, drawing each tit deeply into his mouth.

He entered her swiftly, and she hitched in a deep breath, running her hands down his sweat-slick back. With his body bucking against hers, his penis probing deeper with every stroke, she knew Anthony had her completely under his control, that she would relish every moment.

The iron bed tapped out their hot and frantic rhythm of love against the wall. She lifted her hips, allowing him to go deeper, faster, submitting to the pleasure.

Suddenly, his body stilled, and she drew his face into

the soft curve of her neck, reveling in the long, agonizing groan of their mutual release.

He collapsed in her arms, now softening inside her, breathing hard, and she kissed the top of his head.

"Liza…"

"Shh…don't say anything. I just want you to hold me."

He rolled over next to her and gathered her into his arms. She snuggled against him and closed her eyes.

Suddenly, she heard his phone vibrating on the floor.

Anthony reached down and fumbled around for his suit jacket. He grabbed his phone and cursed under his breath.

Liza draped her arm over her forehead and stared up at him while he looked at the screen.

"Duty calls?" she inquired, trying to keep the disappointment from her voice.

"I'm sorry, Liza," he nodded, sounding frustrated.

He got out of the bed and stood up. "That emergency I was talking about earlier, it's happening now. The patient is being airlifted to the hospital and will arrive soon. I've got to go."

She turned over and faced him, propping her head in the palm of her hand.

"Bad timing. Maybe it's a sign."

Anthony hurried into his clothes and knelt by the side of her bed. "Only that we should continue where we left off, and soon. Meet me at the beach, tomorrow at six a.m."

She groaned and smiled. "Another early-morning meeting?"

He clasped her cheeks between his palms and gave

her a lingering kiss. "I promise you I'll make it worth your while."

She closed her eyes, trying to hold on to the tender moment, and when she finally opened them, he was gone.

Chapter 11

The next morning, Liza woke up feeling like she had the best sleep in her life. Anthony's lovemaking had drifted from her bed right into her dreams. As a result, the tenuous hold she'd had on the lock to her heart was slowly eroding. And by the way he was pleasuring her body last night, she wondered if the same thing was happening to him.

What was it about his lips that carried her into another dimension? His hands that caressed her as if she were made of the finest silk? His tongue probing her body, as if seeking some hidden treasure?

Liza sunk deeper under her covers and clenched her thighs together. The man drove her wild and he wasn't even in the room.

More than anything, Liza wanted Anthony to make

love to her again and again, regardless of the consequences.

She rolled over and looked at the clock. "Six thirty! I'm late!"

Liza stumbled out of bed, hop-skipped over to her dresser and starting pulling on her clothes. She was supposed to meet Anthony at the beach at 6 a.m. sharp. There wasn't even time for a shower, let alone breakfast. She'd have to grab both later.

She was on her way downstairs when she heard her phone ringing, way back in her room where she'd left it on accident.

She ran back upstairs, flipped the phone over and saw that it was Anthony. Rather than let the call go to voice mail, she answered it, ready to face the music.

She opened her mouth, ready to apologize profusely, but Anthony spoke first.

"Did you get my message?"

"No," she responded, sheepishly.

"Where are you? At the beach?"

She rubbed her eyes and stifled a yawn. "Actually, I just rolled out of bed. Where are you?"

"I got called into surgery early this morning and I'm still at the hospital."

"Did you ever get home last night?"

"No, and I never made it to the beach either."

"I'm glad I didn't get your message and slept in," she joked, but there was no laughter on the other end of the phone.

"Listen, I need to see you today. It's about last night."

Liza felt her stomach drop. His voice had a slight edge to it and he sounded tense and worried.

"I should be done here around three. Can you stop by my condo around four, so we can talk?"

She agreed to meet him at his place, ended the call and flopped back on the bed.

Had last night been a mistake?

Her eyes welled with tears, and she tossed her head back and forth, allowing them to flow down her cheeks.

He's running away. He never intended to meet me at the beach.

She had hoped to broach the subject about a long-term relationship, but it seemed as though he didn't want a commitment at all.

She shot out of bed and went to the mirror. Staring at her reflection, Liza saw a woman who was tired of believing the spiteful words of her mother that had been drilled into her head since she was a teen. Tired of worrying about her scar and the rest of her so-called flaws, and what men thought of them, especially Anthony.

Liza knew in her heart that she was a beautiful person, inside and out, and it was about time that she believed it, without the need for a man to tell her so.

She angrily rubbed the tears from her eyes. Once again, she'd been played. But this time, she vowed, would be the last time.

During her long, hot shower, Liza decided that she couldn't face Maisie that morning. The last thing she needed was a round of questioning about her whereabouts the previous evening, despite her host's best intentions.

She decided to have breakfast at Ruby's, before her meeting with Trent at City Hall.

Liza chose her outfit carefully, ultimately deciding to wear one of her favorite cotton sundresses in periwinkle blue.

Though she missed Denver, she loved living in Northern California and the sunny weather often lifted her spirits. The fact that she didn't have to cloister herself in sweaters and coats was a definite plus.

When she was dressed, she grabbed her purse and headed back downstairs. She was halfway there when she decided to go back and get her laptop. After meeting with Trent, she'd head to the library and continue her work on the design of her own home. It would be a busy day, but it would help to keep her mind off of Anthony until it was time to meet him.

Liza had her hand on the front doorknob when Maisie emerged from the parlor.

"Morning! Where did you two slip off to last night?" she asked, waggling a finger. "And don't think I didn't notice."

Liza decided to ignore her question. She turned around and smiled sweetly. "Did Prentice walk you home?"

"He sure did, after I slapped him on the back to wake him up. I swear that man sleeps more than the dead."

"There must be some reason he's tired," Liza teased.

"If there is, it doesn't have anything to do with me. I'm too old for any hanky-panky shenanigans."

She folded her arms, rested them on her bosom and a tiny smile crossed her face.

Liza gave Maisie a hug. "Okay, if you say so."

"By the way, you missed me cutting the ribbon!" she said, sounding hurt.

"I'm sorry," Liza said, with a twinge of guilt for skipping out on her friend. "It was a well-deserved honor."

"Hush, I'm no better than anyone else," Maisie said, waving her comment away. "But stop distracting me. What about you and Anthony? I know I'm not your mama, but don't think you're going to leave this house without telling me where you two snuck off."

Liza discreetly bit the inside of her lip.

Maisie was as sharp as a bat. However, she didn't know that Anthony was in the bed-and-breakfast last night, let alone up in Liza's room. Though she knew Maisie would never intentionally hurt her, Liza just wanted to keep even the smallest details of her relationship with Anthony to herself.

"He walked me here and then had to leave right away because he got called to the hospital on an emergency," she lied.

Maisie lifted a brow. "Any clue on what happened?"

Liza shook her head. "I can only imagine it must have been serious. The patient arrived by helicopter. Anthony once told me he is often called to assist when there has been an injury that is disfiguring or has the potential to be disfiguring, like bad burns that require skin grafts."

Maisie frowned. "It must not have been a Bay Pointer, or one of us would have surely heard about it by now." She patted Liza's hand. "There will be other times for you and Anthony to talk, not to worry."

Liza faked a smile and gave her a quick hug. "Who's worried?" she said, before scooting out the door.

Upon arriving at Ruby's, Liza headed straight to the counter to order her breakfast and then selected a table on the patio, hoping the fresh air would help to clear her head.

She rubbed her forehead, as if that would help drive thoughts of Anthony away. She looked across the street to the town square, and was surprised to see that the Bay Point Carousel was running.

At this hour of the morning, the twinkly music was a shock to her system. It was like hearing the jingle of the ice cream truck at the wrong time of the day, or worse, when you didn't have any money.

Ruby sailed by with Liza's latte and food. Today, she'd chosen a scone over a croissant.

Liza jerked a thumb in the direction of the square. "It's too early for something to sound so happy," she half whined.

Ruby looked over and nodded. "Then never come here on a Thursday morning, because that's when they tinker with that old thing," she advised.

Liza lightly tapped one finger on her scone. Though she knew it would probably taste delicious, it seemed as hard as her attitude.

"I thought the renovation was finished," she said, barely hiding a scowl.

"All that pretty, historically accurate paint and sparkling lights can't hide the fact that the carousel is over one hundred years old, with the creaks and cracks to prove it."

The annoyingly cheery music of the carousel rang out through the square, but she was determined to ignore it.

At best, it reminded her of her childhood, which though rich in possessions, was devoid of consistent love and acceptance.

Her father was a surgeon and rarely at home. Though he was a kind and generous man, she never got the sense that she mattered in his life. While her mother was more focused on maintaining her youth through endless cosmetic treatments than caring for Liza.

At worst, the carousel reminded her how happiness could be faked. And when the ride was over, the disappointment seemed to last forever.

Liza felt her eyes moisten. Her growing affection for Anthony had made her happier than she'd been in a very long time, but she had a feeling he was about to break her heart.

"I hope that if I make it to that age, I get that much attention," she said, doing her best to smile.

Ruby laughed. "You and me both, honey."

When Ruby left, Liza bit into her scone and found that it was very tasty. She turned on her phone and frowned, half hoping to see a text from Anthony, but her screen was blank.

"Might as well catch up on my overflowing inbox," she mumbled to herself.

Liza was so engrossed in reading email on her phone

that it wasn't until thirty minutes later that she looked up and realized that the patio was filled with townspeople. She spotted Mariella Vency, Mayor Langston's executive assistant, scanning the crowd looking for a seat, and motioned her over. She'd met the woman several weeks earlier when she inquired about construction permits.

Mariella approached, a tentative smile on her face. "I can't believe all the tables are full so early. Are you sure you don't mind sharing?"

"Not at all." Liza began to rise from her seat. "I was actually going to order another latte. If you wouldn't mind waiting here, I can get yours at the same time, if you'd like."

"Don't get up," Mariella gushed. "Coffee is on me. It's my thanks for letting me barge in on you like this."

Before Liza could refuse her kindness, Mariella disappeared inside.

In the meantime, she finished reading an email, and had just stowed her phone away in her purse, when Mariella returned.

"Hope you don't mind the to-go cups."

Liza smiled as she accepted one from Mariella's outstretched hand. "It's fine. Thanks again."

Mariella sat down and blew out a breath. "I can only sit here for a little while before I have to go to work."

"Do you enjoy it?"

"It's definitely interesting working for Mayor Langston, especially now," she replied.

Liza took a careful sip of the hot brew. "Watching

his plan for redeveloping downtown Bay Point come together?"

Mariella nodded. "I was so excited when he was re-elected, especially since I got to keep my job. If they'd voted for the other guy, I would have been out for sure."

They were under a patio umbrella, but Mariella's sun-kissed caramel-colored skin glowed so perfectly that it made Liza momentarily envious, until she spotted sadness lurking in her eyes.

"Are you married?"

Mariella laughed. "Oh no. My son Josh calls me 'unhappily' single."

She sobered, frowned. "I try not to let it show how much it sometimes sucks to be single, but it seems as though he can read my mind."

"I'm not a parent, but I can only imagine how tough it can be."

"Sometimes I feel he would be better off with a male role model, but just between us girls, so far, there's been no prospects."

Mariella tapped the plastic cover of her cup. "But I shouldn't complain. I moved to Bay Point for peace, quiet and the school system, not the men. Although, there are more than a few hotties living here. Dr. Marbet is one example, wouldn't you agree?"

Liza froze, not knowing what to say, wondering if she knew anything about their relationship, other than that in the eyes of the public, it was strictly business.

After last night, she and Anthony were now lovers. But how long would they remain so?

"I really hadn't noticed." She pulled out her phone

and swiped it on. "I'm so sorry, but I'm expected in a meeting."

Mariella put her hand over her mouth. "Oh gosh. I'm sorry. I hope I haven't made you late with my rambling."

"It's no problem. My meeting is at City Hall. I hope to break ground on Dr. Marbet's clinic sooner versus later so I'm meeting with Trent Waterson and the building inspector to finalize permits for the project."

Liza dropped her phone back into her purse and made sure her laptop case was zipped up.

"Do you know Trent?" she asking, thinking he might just be the 'hot prospect' Mariella needed.

"Yes, I do. He's a good guy, but totally not my type. I'm not into guys on motorcycles. They're too dangerous."

"Who? The guys or the motorcycles?"

"Both," Mariella giggled, as she lifted her cup and shouldered her own purse. "Let's go."

The two women strolled over to City Hall. They were climbing the stairs when Liza stopped and snapped her fingers.

"What do you say we have a girls' night out sometime?"

Mariella's eyes widened, and Liza could almost see her mulling the idea over in her head.

"It sounds like fun, but I don't know if I could leave Josh alone."

"How old is he?"

"Almost fifteen," she replied. "But I still don't like leaving him alone. I guess you could say I'm just a little bit overprotective."

Liza wanted to roll her eyes, but held back, knowing she had no right to judge. "I think you could use a few hours away."

"It's been a long time," Mariella agreed.

"Plus, it will give us a chance to get to know each other," Liza gushed, hoping she didn't sound overeager. "I don't have many friends here yet."

"Nor do I, even though I've lived here for a couple of years," Mariella admitted, with a wide grin. "Between work and taking care of Josh, I tend to forget about myself."

Liza grinned. "Then it's all settled." She bumped her shoulder gently against Mariella's. "Girls rule!"

There's nothing like making a new friend to help one get over heartbreak, Liza thought, as they walked into City Hall.

"So I know this cute little roadhouse just outside of town that has live music and dancing…"

Chapter 12

Liza stared down at her phone as a text message from Anthony slid across the screen.

Door is open. Just walk in.

She stared at her reflection in the mirror, and for once, she didn't lift her jaw to check on her scar.

I could ignore or delete the text, she thought, picking up her brush and running it through her hair.

But she didn't want to ignore it, or her feelings for Anthony.

Satisfied that her hair looked okay, she set her brush down on her dresser and smoothed the wrinkles from her dress.

Despite her best efforts, her mind kept wandering

toward Anthony, as it had throughout the day, and what was inevitably waiting for her if she met up with him.

It was why after her meeting with Trent she'd decided to return to the bed-and-breakfast instead of going to the library. In case Anthony didn't contact her, she could simply flop into bed and cry her eyes out.

But he did, and though she was sure she was going to regret it, she decided to meet him and face whatever it was he had to say.

Maisie had left a note that she had gone to a late lunch with some friends from church, but would return soon, as she was expecting guests to arrive in the early evening.

Liza grabbed her keys and a white straw hat to protect her face from the sun, and hurried down the stairs.

As she walked to Anthony's condo, she tried to talk herself into turning on her heels and heading back to her room at Maisie's. But she couldn't face Maisie's questions either.

When she arrived, she started knocking on the door, but remembered it was already unlocked. Before she could change her mind, she took a deep breath and opened it.

The entryway opened up to a great room with a cathedral ceiling. She looked up and saw that the transom windows were open, and felt a hint of breeze on her cheeks.

The late-afternoon sun streamed into the room and cast a warm glow on the leather furniture. Soft jazz was playing, though she couldn't see any speakers.

But where was Anthony?

She shut the door and clutched her keys tightly, heels clicking on the varnished wooden floor as she walked.

"Hello?" she called out.

"Be right down!"

Liza followed the sound of his deep voice and discovered a staircase that led to the second floor.

"Make yourself comfortable. I'll be there in a minute."

The soft whoosh of the two ceiling fans created a relaxing environment. She plopped down on the couch and nestled her keys in her lap, rubbing her bare arms against the breeze.

Suddenly, she heard a door slam, followed by a string of curses.

Liza swiveled her head and watched Anthony hurry down the stairs.

He leaned down and pecked her cheek. "Sorry I'm late," he said, a sheepish grin on his face.

"I hadn't noticed," she replied in an off-handed way. "I'm sure what you have to say won't take long."

His chasteness bothered her. After the passion they had shared last night, she wondered why he didn't give her a full-on kiss.

She met his eyes, and saw that he was watching her intently.

"You said you wanted to talk about last night, so talk."

Anthony gave her a curious look and sat down next to her. "Before we get to that, weren't you supposed to meet with Trent today?"

She nodded. "We met at City Hall this morning. The

permits are all in order. The motel will be razed next week."

Anthony raised a fist, as if victorious. "Bring in the dozers and bring out the dirt!"

Liza couldn't help but smile briefly at his antics. However, she saw no reason to postpone the inevitable.

"Now, what did you want to talk about?"

She fought not to let her eyes roam his body. Though he was dressed casually in a white T-shirt and navy blue basketball shorts, how was she supposed to have a normal conversation with the man when he looked good enough to eat?

Instead, she mentally braced herself for the news that she feared. That the previous night had been a mistake. That he regretted making love to her.

Anthony avoided her eyes and looked at the floor. "It was very tough leaving you last night, unlike anything I've ever faced before."

He rubbed his free hand across the back of his neck. "Last night was…incredible. But I don't know what to do next or where this will lead."

Liza met his eyes, and saw indecision. A wellspring of hurt sprung forth. Though she loved him, she knew exactly what she had to do to save her own heart. She had to end the relationship first.

She swallowed away a lump in her throat. "It's okay, Anthony. I understand."

His eyes narrowed. "What do you mean, you *understand*?"

Liza folded her arms, and she accidentally jabbed one of her keys into her bare skin. She bit her lip against the pain. "I don't know why you are wasting my time, Anthony. You could have just told me you didn't want to see me anymore over the phone!"

"You've got it all wrong, Liza," he said, leaning in close to her. She shivered when he placed his arm around her shoulders.

He took her hand and she hitched in a gasp when he placed it squarely in the middle of his shorts. She'd been so busy feeling sorry for herself that she hadn't noticed his erection.

"Does this look like I don't want to see you anymore?"

She held her hand still and bit her lip, knowing what she wanted to do, not knowing if she dared.

Liza sucked in a breath, then slowly reached over and tentatively slid her hand beneath his shorts.

She bit her lip again.

He wore no underwear.

She touched the silky tip of his engorged penis, discovered a bead of moisture there, barely aware that he was bending his head toward her, closing the gap between them, until she felt his finger lift her chin.

Liza met his eyes briefly, and saw the heat of desire in them. This was a man who wanted her, not someone who wanted to throw away what was just beginning.

But she had to be sure.

He rubbed the pad of his thumb over her bottom lip, forcing her to look into his eyes.

"Well, does it?" he demanded softly.

She closed her eyes and shook her head. He was sexually attracted to her. That much was obvious, but she wanted more than just a brief fling with Anthony. What that meant, she didn't know.

"No, it certainly doesn't. But what does your heart say?"

Anthony didn't say a word, but lifted her right hand and slowly kissed each and every knuckle.

"It says I want you. It says I need you."

Does it say that you love me? she wanted to ask, but she didn't dare. The tender moment would have broken, the answer perhaps not want she wanted to hear.

No, she decided to herself, this was better. The exquisite joy of discovery, the painful longing to be with him, the angst of waiting, would all be worth it in the end.

At least she hoped so.

His penis throbbed against her hand, so velvety and hot to the touch that she wanted to purr.

"Maybe our hearts are speaking the same language?" she whispered, as she gazed into his eyes. "What do you think, Doctor?"

Anthony kissed the side of her neck. "Only one way to find out."

His lips brushed against hers, softly teasing her mouth open until her tongue darted out, curious and brazen.

Without breaking contact from her mouth, he placed his warm hands lightly on both sides of her head, fingers splayed into her hair.

Liza slid her hands around his waist, succumbing. Her mouth parted, her heart completely open to him.

Anthony kissed her deeply, lovingly, possessing her

lips, inciting the dark spirit of her passion as they sank back onto the sofa.

She reached between them, trying to grab hold of his penis, trying to claim what was now hers. He grunted and stood up, and she stretched catlike, watching him disrobe.

There were no curtains and no blinds on the large windows of the great room. She felt herself moisten with the thought that someone might be watching them make sweet afternoon love.

She turned on her side and gasped as Anthony lay beside her, his warm body aligning with hers. She felt herself tremble when he gathered her in his arms.

"This sofa is so narrow," she whispered as she slipped her hands around his waist and drew him closer. But really, it wasn't narrow at all. She just preferred to be as close to him as possible, but felt too shy at the moment to tell him.

His erection thumped against her fully clothed belly, and she yearned to grab hold of it again, and feel it against her own skin and never let go.

She held back, and instead, her hands boldly rounded his bare, round buttocks, and his muscles tightened in response.

"Liza…" he groaned as he rolled on top of her.

She traced a finger slowly up his spine, drawing a series of short gasps from him, and she began to massage his right buttock with her other hand.

His eyes were closed, as if he was dreaming, and he seemed content to stroke his hand through her hair, keeping his lips hovering near hers.

The subtle heat made her cheeks flush, and not able to wait any longer, her hands left his back and buttocks, and she brought his face to fully meet hers.

Their kisses lengthened with every minute that passed, and her heart thudded in her chest so hard she was sure he could feel it.

Suddenly, he stopped and lifted his body up from hers. When he stood, she panicked momentarily.

"What's wrong?" she asked, barely able to keep her eyes off his rock-hard abdomen.

"Nothing, I just want you right here."

Liza bent towards his engorged flesh and opened her mouth, then cried out when he swiftly picked her up by the waist, and gave her another kiss.

She giggled and wrapped her legs tightly around his waist.

"Bad girl," he teased, slapping her ass lightly.

She held on tight to his neck and kissed him back, enjoying the feel as his hands slipped under her dress and over her white cotton bikini. He slid one finger, then two along the waistband, as if asking permission to remove them.

Though Liza wiggled to help him, the position was awkward and she didn't want to release her thighs from his waist. So he snuck his hands under her panties and he cupped her buttocks.

The pads of his fingers flexed and pressed into her bare skin, and she moaned with pleasure at the feel of his hands and the sound of fabric ripping.

But her sundress was caught between them, an unwanted barrier that frustrated her. So she wiggled again in his arms and finally he caught on, reaching one hand up her back.

She held on tight as he drew her zipper down while kissing her hard, driving his tongue into her mouth. Like a viper, it met with her own, hot and wet, sweeping and sinking deeper. She allowed him no constraints, stretching her limits, widening her passion.

She wanted more. So much more.

Liza moaned and clenched her thighs even tighter around his hips, as the low, decadent sound of a saxophone filtered through the room.

She broke away from him, raising her arms briefly, so he could remove her sundress. Anthony swiveled on his heels and hitched her up higher on his hips.

The wet crotch of her panties, hot and moist, slid against his long, hard flesh and she longed to be completely naked against him. Longed for him to be inside her, moving within, taking possession, like he had the night before.

She thought he would take her right there, in the open living room, but he suddenly turned on his bare feet.

"Hold on," he murmured low into her ear.

She closed her eyes and did as he asked, anchoring her arms around his neck, tightening her legs around his hips, buffered by his large hands gripping the backs of her upper thighs.

Anthony laid her gently on his bed, and then slowly slipped off her underwear. He nuzzled her neck until she laughed aloud and begged him to stop, tears streaming out of her eyes.

His lips came next, planting tender new memories wherever they landed on her sensitive skin.

Suddenly, she surprised him with a long and lingering kiss that spoke the loving words she didn't have the courage to say.

When she was done, he flopped back against the pillow and uttered a slow whistle.

"Whoa. That was some kiss. What was that about?"

She propped herself up on one elbow, and grinned at him.

"I'm the kind of woman who takes what she wants."

He caressed the underside of one breast, watching her eyes. "What do you mean?"

Liza took a long look at the man lying before her. He was hard as a rock and ripe for straddling. She licked her lips, closed her palm at the base of his thick flesh, and slowly positioned herself over his hips.

"Why don't I just show you?" she said in a low, sexy tone, as she eased his shaft into her body.

She began to rock slowly back and forth, then up and down, varying the rhythm and the intensity.

He got up on both elbows and laved at the nipple of her left breast, then her right, drawing each into his mouth and lovingly sucking each one, as she arched her back, and begged for more.

Finally, still inside her, he settled back on the pillow and his hands rounded her ass. She held back a scream of pleasure as he thrust up into her with a loud grunt, piercing her.

"I'm giving you control, baby. I'm just gonna hold on."

She steadied her hands on his shoulders and tightened her core. The freedom to do what she wanted made her move upon him even faster, gaining heat, gaining friction, until she suddenly cried out.

Together they shattered…and soared.

Liza woke up; her mind was in a complete fog. For a moment, she didn't know if it was the same day or a different day. Then she felt a hand gently brushing a few strands of hair from her forehead, then a soft kiss.

She shivered with delight and remembered.

She was with Anthony Marbet, the man she loved.

And the thought scared her to death.

Liza turned over on her side, away from his embrace.

"I don't know if I'm going to be able to look at you fully clothed the same way again," she said, reaching down to pull the covers over her naked body.

"And that's a bad thing?" He got up on one elbow, leaned over and kissed her shoulder. "Because to tell you the truth? I could get used to this."

She ignored him, but kept on pulling, feeling her breasts jiggle with the effort.

Finally, she stopped, propped herself up by the elbows to have a look. Somehow the sheet had gotten wound around his right lower calf. And by the grin on his face, the man wasn't letting go.

Liza gave up and flopped back against the pillow.

"What do you mean by 'this'?" she asked.

He trailed a finger down the cleft between her breasts, and she felt her nipples stiffen.

"Seeing you. Naked in my bed. I love it."

"I love it, too."

He bent over and licked each hard tip, just once, in response.

But do you love me? she wanted to ask, as she held back a moan from the heat of his tongue.

She watched Anthony kick the sheets off his legs, and then looked into his eyes and held her breath. It seemed as though he were waiting for her to decide the next move.

But she didn't want to think about the future, or even tomorrow.

And when he pulled her close to him, right where she wanted to be, she breathed again and felt complete.

In the third afterglow of their lovemaking, Liza stretched like a cat in Anthony's arms, but she was by no means tired. Her knuckle brushed against the side of her jaw, grazing her scar, and her heart sank.

He hadn't said a thing about her scar, not last night, not ever. But why?

Perhaps she should be glad that he didn't, but on the other hand, it bothered her that he didn't care enough to ask. She wanted to hear him say that her scar didn't bother him, that he liked her, or better yet, loved her, in spite of her flaws.

Her mind would have swirled on, but Anthony's voice reeled her back into reality.

"Oh crap, I have to be at the hospital in thirty minutes. Night shift." He swung his legs over the side of the bed and turned back to look at her. "See, baby, you are already messing with my schedule."

He started to reach toward his phone on the night

table, but she stopped him and frowned. "We always seem to get interrupted, don't we?"

He cupped her cheek. "Listen, Liza, I can separate this pretty easily from everything else," he said, matter-of-factly. "From my job, from the building project, from all the other bullcrap in my life."

She listened to his words, and at the same time, tried to figure out the meaning behind them.

He tugged lightly at her chin, forcing her to look into his eyes.

"This is my space, our space, to enjoy and pleasure each other with no limits and no commitment."

No commitment.

The unexpected shock of those two words felt like a bucket of cold water dumped from behind. The one thing she feared, the realization that Anthony would not want a commitment, was happening.

Men are players—from the very beginning—get used to it.

The harsh words of her mother replayed in her mind, and once again, she struggled with discouraging thoughts.

She squeezed her eyes shut, willing away the tears.

Anthony was a cosmetic surgeon, in the business of cultivating perfection. She would never be perfect, surely he realized that, and yet, it felt as if he were rejecting her. The sting of hurt was worse now that they'd made love, not once, but multiple times.

Liza had read in a book once that men could compartmentalize their feelings, which made her think of a row of safe-deposit boxes at a bank. All heavily guarded, locked down. Only able to be opened in a private room, with a key.

There was a treasure trove of pleasure to be had in Anthony's bedroom, but what she really wanted was his heart.

"No commitment, huh?" she said, opening her eyes and forcing her voice to sound light and airy. "Can I consider our contract broken?"

"Only if you want to be sued by kisses."

Liza couldn't tell if he was serious or just playing along. But before she could ask, he leaned over and gave her a quick kiss. "I'm headed for the shower."

She trailed a finger down his chest. "Can I join you?"

He shook his head. "I wish, but I don't want to be late. Can I get a rain check?"

Liza hid her disappointment behind a smile and watched as his fine, muscular body exited into the adjoining bathroom. The very image of seeing him wet and sexy in a towel made her suck in her breath.

Liza dressed quickly, long enough to hear Anthony humming in the shower, a song she recognized from the nineties. The male singer had died too soon, yet he'd left a legacy of music that had sparked many a love affair.

Maybe it was a sign, or maybe he just liked old-school jams.

You can't measure a lifetime in one night, the singer crooned.

She laughed bitterly, realizing how true the lyrics were in her own situation, and tears filled her eyes.

Before leaving, she texted him a quick note.

Had fun. Going home to take a shower. TTYL?

She stared at the question mark in her text. It reflected how she felt about her and Anthony's relationship at the moment.

Lots of questions and no easy answers.

Chapter 13

At 7 a.m. the next morning, Anthony returned home, fatigued and famished. All he wanted to do was grab a quick bowl of cereal, watch a bit of the morning news and then crash into bed.

He straggled into his condo and shut the door.

"It's about time you got here," Doc Z shouted. "I've been waiting up for you all night."

"You really didn't have to do that, Doc," Anthony said. He tossed his keys onto the entrance hall table and glanced at his reflection in the mirror above.

I'm a big boy.

Liza had said as much last night, when they had made love. He grinned, remembering the sound of her teasing, sensual voice, which had quickly turned into moans when she'd taken him in her mouth.

Anthony remembered it all in vivid detail. The memories of making love to Liza had helped to keep him awake, and at the same time, were the perfect fodder for the guilt that had plagued him all night long.

He'd hated leaving her last night, and the time before, but there was nothing he could do. He was a doctor and his patients were his first priority. Now he wondered just how long it would take Liza to get tired of him.

He knew his track record with women. Most couldn't understand his ambition and his need to help people. But deep down, he knew that Liza was different. She was good for him, and that's what scared him the most.

Anthony sighed, kicked off his shoes and walked into the great room.

"You're in my chair," he said in a half-joking tone.

Doc turned in his seat and used the remote to mute the television.

"What did I do?" he blurted out, as if offended. "I sat down, flipped up the recliner and fell asleep waiting for you."

Anthony sank down into a second recliner, which was identical to "his" favorite chair, but didn't have the same feel.

"You could have gone to bed."

Doc laughed. "And miss the chance to bust your chops? No way!" He switched off the television. "Besides, I figure you owe me, after what I did for you last night."

Anthony raised a brow. "By staying out of sight?"

"Yeah." Doc took a sip out of his coffee cup. "Want some? It's fresh and hot."

He shook his head. "No. The plan is to go to sleep,

not stay awake. But I appreciate the offer, and the time alone last night."

"But I take it you weren't alone for long," Doc insinuated, with a slow grin.

"No, Liza stopped by," Anthony responded, deliberately being vague.

"And?" Doc prompted.

He shrugged. "We talked."

Anthony watched him get up, walk over to the minibar and pour himself another cup of coffee.

Doc turned. "You better do more than talk to keep a woman like Liza happy."

He glanced over at his friend and mentor. "What do you mean by that?"

"All I'm saying is, don't make the same mistakes I did," Doc advised when he returned to his seat. "I had a great career and I've got a lot of material possessions to show for it. I only wish I had a woman to enjoy it all with."

Anthony pushed down on the lever and his chair leaned back. He settled back, remembering the feel of Liza in his arms. She was an amazing lover, and though he didn't know much about her personally, he wanted to know more.

However, if he decided to pursue a serious relationship, he had to weigh the risks, not necessarily to him, but to Liza.

"Don't worry. I know what I'm doing, Doc."

But the truth was, he had no idea at all.

Liza gingerly stepped out of the shower. Though she'd had a restful sleep, her legs were still wobbly from the evening of lovemaking with Anthony. But it was the kind of ache she never wanted to go away.

What that man did to her body! And she'd loved every single, thigh-bumping, hip-slapping, lip-biting moment.

Though she didn't know what lay ahead, she still hoped that they would see each other as often as their crazy schedules allowed. While he was busy at the hospital, she would keep busy ensuring that the construction of his clinic went smoothly.

Word was starting to get around about her one-woman architecture firm, and she'd had more interest from potential clients than she could handle right now. She felt bad turning down work, but her first priority was the clinic, and then other projects, including working with the historical society on the renovation of the old Bay Point School House.

Liza knew now that she had made the right choice to move to Bay Point. But she still had doubts about her relationship with Anthony. She knew he cared about her, he'd told her so countless times, but there was still something missing. The feeling of permanence.

At any moment, either one of them could decide that whatever they shared could end. That it wasn't worth it; they'd had their fill of one another. That there was nothing left to give, and nothing left to receive.

She prayed that would never, ever happen, but it was always a possibility.

It was Sunday morning, and the sun had just risen. Maisie would be up and about making breakfast and

Liza was starving, so she dressed, grabbed her phone and headed downstairs to the kitchen.

"Good morning," she said, cheerfully.

"Well! Look what set with the moon and rose with the sun. I missed you at dinner last night. We had a pretty lively crew."

She smiled weakly. "Does nothing get past you?"

"Not usually, but no need to explain. This is one situation that is none of my business."

Maisie raised her hand. "Besides, I can see it all over your face," she continued. "I used to have a similar look after a night of good loving with my late husband. That man would rock me into the next county over."

She doubled over with laughter, her head swaying back and forth. "God, he was good."

"Shh," Liza warned, mortified. "What about your other guests? What if they hear you?"

Maisie wiped the tears from her eyes. "A couple checked out yesterday, remember? As for the remaining guests, I'm assuming they're not early risers, like you and I."

Liza shook her head. "I guess I forgot."

Maisie tapped the side of her head with one finger. "Just another sign you've got a doctor on the brain."

She hid a smile of amazement. *Did the woman know everything?*

Maisie held up her palm, interrupting her thoughts. "Forgetfulness must be catching. I just remembered you got a message from Shelby last night."

Liza raised a brow and followed Maisie to the small reception desk just outside the parlor, hoping nothing was wrong. Shelby was her best friend from college. She was scheduled to visit soon and Liza couldn't wait to see her again.

"She called twice last night," Maisie said, squinting. "She says she lost her cell phone and all her contacts, but she'll give you a call when she gets a new one." She looked up. "That's the one who will be here in a few weeks, right?"

Liza nodded. "Yes. Thanks so much for letting her stay here. As I said, I'll cover the cost of her room."

Shelby had lost her job several months prior and hadn't been able to find a new one. She was driving cross-country job hunting and sightseeing at the same time. Liza didn't like the thought of her being alone, without a phone or a way to contact anyone.

Maisie smiled. "No problem. I'll just add it to your bill."

She looked Liza up and down. "I swear, girl, ever since you've been seeing the good doctor, you've been getting skinnier and skinnier. Join an old woman for breakfast, won't you?"

Liza nodded, and they went back into the kitchen.

Maisie's delicious home cooking would take her mind off Anthony, at least for a little while.

She headed for the coffeemaker, poured two cups, put two heaping spoons of sugar into one just the way Maisie liked it and set both on the table.

She watched as Maisie laid wide strips of bacon on the griddle.

"Anything I can do to help?"

Maisie scooped flour into a large blue bowl. "Melt a couple of pats of butter in the microwave for me."

Liza did as she was asked and as the ministrations of making breakfast proceeded, little was said between the two women.

She took over cooking the bacon, watching it pop and crackle, and making sure that none of the residual grease ended up on her clothes or skin. When it was done, she carefully laid each slice side-by-side on a paper towel.

Liza sat down and took a sip of her coffee. "Do you mind if I ask you something?"

Maisie poured some milk into a large blue bowl, added flour and began stirring. "Sure, honey. What is it?"

"How do you know when a man really loves you?"

Maisie set down her spoon, and sat next to her.

"I was married almost fifty years to my husband, and he loved me till his dying day. I had a lot of flaws. One in particular, like talking too much."

Maisie laughed. "When the thing you think will drive him away is what actually brings you together," she said, patting her hand. "That's when you'll know."

Liza smiled, and knew in her heart Maisie was right. It was time to stop worrying about the future and enjoy her relationship with Anthony right now.

"Did anyone ever tell you that you give the best advice?"

"What are friends for?" she said, with a smile.

Liza's phone buzzed. She swiped it on and saw that she had a text message from Anthony.

Late dinner tonight?

Her heart skipped a beat, and she paused, fingers hovering over her phone, as she considered her response.

Yes. When and what time?

Lucy's. Back patio. 9 p.m.

I'll be there.

Liza wrung her hands in anticipation. She hadn't expected to see him so soon, but their date tonight was further proof that he missed and cared about her.

"Good news?"

She looked up and nodded. "I hope so." Remembering Maisie's advice, she smiled brightly. "I know so."

"That's what I like to hear."

Maisie set down a platter of blueberry pancakes and bacon. "Now eat a good breakfast. Falling in love takes lots of energy."

And a lot of courage, Liza thought, and dug in.

"How's the roast chicken?" Anthony asked. He felt like a heel, asking such an inane question, but ever since Liza had arrived, he'd been strangely tongue-tied.

And oddly enough, so had she.

Conversation had been stilted during the appetizer phase of the meal, and completely shut down during the main course.

She met his eyes. "It's fine, Anthony."

Maybe she's just hungry, he thought, but she had barely touched her food.

"Do you have to go to the hospital tonight?"

He shook his head. "No, not since I worked last night."

She reached for his hand. "Maybe after dinner, we can go back to your place?"

She gave him a sexy smile that made him reconsider for a moment what he was about to say, but then he came to his senses.

He shook his head. "No, not tonight Liza."

It was like they were playing some cat-and-mouse game. Still, he couldn't ignore the hurt look in her eyes.

"Is it…because of me?" she asked. "Or something about me?"

He sat back in his chair, glad that he'd specifically reserved the back patio. He knew their conversation would turn personal at some point, and he didn't want any prying ears or eyes.

"No, not at all."

Liza fiddled with her fork, and he thought she was satisfied with his answer. So he took a sip of his wine, and began to finish his meal.

In a way, he was glad for the silence. He felt comfortable in it.

Suddenly, Liza pushed back her plate and blurted, "Why haven't you ever asked me about my scar?"

Anthony looked up, and swallowed in shock. "What scar?"

She turned her face, lifted her hair. "This one," she

said, pointing to the side of her jaw. "Why haven't you ever said anything about it?"

He set down his knife and fork. "Because I don't care about it, but now that you mentioned it, how did it happen?"

Her eyes scanned the table, and then lifted to meet his.

"When I was in college," she began. "I was trying to fit in with everyone, and I went with a few of my friends to a party at a frat house.

"Everyone was drinking too much, and a really good-looking guy started flirting with me. My friends got angry."

"They were jealous," Anthony offered. He wouldn't be surprised. Liza was so beautiful.

She shrugged. "I suppose. Anyway, they started an argument, to draw the guy's attention away from me, I guess. So I left the party alone."

He reached for her hand and squeezed it. At that moment, Liza seemed so unsure of herself, and he wanted her to know that she didn't have to be. He was with her.

Liza took a deep breath. "On the way back to my dorm, a man tried to steal my purse, and when I stupidly tried to hold on to it, he cut me on my jaw."

Anthony drew in a shocked breath. "Oh no, Liza."

"Luckily, my friend Shelby came along looking for me because she was worried. She was the only one of my college friends who wasn't jealous of me. She called the police and the ambulance. If she hadn't come along when she did…"

Her eyes misted over and her voice trailed off. Anthony squeezed her hand again, and waited until she was ready to finish her story.

"Were you hurt badly?"

Liza shook her head. "At first, I thought I was. The cut wasn't serious enough for cosmetic surgery, which made my mother very angry."

Anthony let go of her hand in shock. "Why?"

"She always wanted me to be perfect, with no flaws, especially on my face. She blamed me for the incident, saying that the guy had only been playing games with me. If only I'd realized that, she'd say, the attack wouldn't have happened and it was my fault that I had a scar."

Anthony shook his head, hardly believing that a mother could be so cruel to her own child. But deep down, he knew he shouldn't be surprised. He knew from experience that some people would do anything in the name of beauty.

"The guy was obviously a maniac. Did you ever find out who it was?"

"No. But I've never forgotten him."

He squeezed her hand again, though he wished he could take her into his arms. "I'm so sorry, Liza."

Liza had a faraway look in her eyes, as if she hadn't heard him speaking.

"My mother died about two years ago from complications from cosmetic surgery. She spent her whole life and a ton of money trying to maintain her looks. Though I loved her, I realized, after she was gone, that she never truly loved me."

Anthony felt his heart squeeze in his chest at the

thought of anyone or anything hurting Liza. And at that moment, he knew he was falling in love with her.

"She was wrong, you know. About everything."

"I wish I could believe that, Anthony," she sniffed, and he could see she was trying to hold back tears. "But you're a cosmetic surgeon. You're in the business of beauty, of making people perfect. Don't you expect perfection from me?"

He wanted to take her in his arms, but he held back, knowing now was not the time. He had to wait a little longer. He needed time to think about what his feelings for Liza meant for him, for her and for them.

"No matter what happens, Liza, in my eyes, you'll always be beautiful."

He never felt stronger about his words, which made what he had to say next even harder to do. He looked down at his half-empty plate and folded his hands.

When he looked up, Liza was dabbing at her eyes with her napkin.

"You make it sound as if I'm never going to see you again."

He inhaled a breath. "Of course, we're going to see each other again, but I think we need a break."

Liza shook her head. "But why? I thought we had something good and right and loving."

"We do," he insisted. "I just need some time to process how I feel. Ever since I met you, you've been on my mind constantly, in a good way, but I'm afraid it's going to affect my work. I feel like I'm off-balance in a way, and as a physician, I can't afford to let that happen."

He brought her hand to his lips, and kissed her knuckles. "You understand, don't you?"

Anthony saw her lips quiver, and he couldn't ignore the tears in her eyes. Yet, when she slipped her hand from his and walked out of the restaurant, he did what he came to do.

He let her go.

Chapter 14

Liza gathered her gown and stepped from her truck. She'd had the vehicle washed, but it still looked as though it had been through a dust storm. She ignored the smirk on the valet attendant's face and handed him her keys.

Though construction was far from complete, Mayor Langston was throwing a small gala event at his family's Spanish-style estate to celebrate the groundbreaking of several new Bay Point businesses.

She walked up the redbrick path, lined with eucalyptus and rose bushes.

The home wasn't as large as she'd expected, but was gorgeous nonetheless, with huge windows and a porch on the second floor that looked like it wrapped around the entire house. The front doors were thrown open and she could see people in formal dress milling around.

Her heels were high and her steps were tentative, not with fear, but excitement. Anthony was just one of many owners who were the guests of honor.

She hadn't seen Anthony, other than at the clinic's construction site, for over two months. She missed him terribly, and her body ached with need.

She wasn't even sure she wanted to go to the gala, until Maisie had practically pushed her out the door.

While everyone in town knew about their business relationship, only Maisie had a vague idea about their bedroom romps.

Since they'd agreed to take a break from being lovers and had gone back to being just business partners, he was distant, and it seemed like a storm cloud had rolled in and settled over his head.

Liza bit her lip and entered the open doorway, wondering how he would act around her that evening.

There was a large mirror in the foyer, and since the small entranceway was empty, she turned to view her reflection.

She'd chosen a full-length black gown with a plunging neckline, and had added a gold necklace with a thin, gold arrow pointing directly to her cleavage. Blatantly sexy, yes, but Liza didn't care. Maybe once he saw her in this dress, he'd remember what he was missing.

Liza turned and walked down a hallway with a low, curved ceiling. Pairs of bronze sconces dripping clear-glass crystals flanked the walls, creating a romantic glow. She could hear the low wail of a flügelhorn and the muted slap of an electric bass.

Toward the end of the hallway, she heard Anthony's voice, and hitched in a breath when a woman's voice quickly followed.

On her tiptoes once again, she caught a snippet of conversation and her stomach churned.

"…looks fabulous…" Anthony said.

"It's all for you, honey" the woman cooed. "Your handiwork on display."

Liza peeked around the corner and her brows knit together when she saw Eloise Bradshaw run her hands down the front of her body, then loop her arms around Anthony's neck.

His handiwork.

Eloise must be a former patient of Anthony's, that much she could gather, but what else was she to him?

Liza stepped back and slumped against the wall. She hadn't seen the woman in months. Not since the ribbon cutting at City Hall, when Eloise had been hanging off Anthony like a Christmas ornament.

That night, Anthony had chosen to go home with her, not Eloise, yet the woman was still trying to poach her man.

She jerked her chin up. *Maybe because Eloise doesn't know Anthony is mine*, she thought.

She chanced a peek around the corner and saw Eloise, her arms still around his neck, and her large, obviously fake, breasts pressed against his tuxedo.

"Oh, hell no!" she muttered under her breath, before sweeping into the small courtyard.

Eloise and Anthony were only a few feet away, standing in front of a bubbling fountain.

"Excuse me, do either of you know where the ladies' room is?"

Her voice seemed to bounce off the walls of the room, but at that moment, she didn't care.

Anthony turned around, a surprised look on his face, and he pushed Eloise's arms away, as if they were on fire.

She watched with internal glee as Eloise stepped back, narrowed her eyes and glared at her, and then at Anthony, who looked visibly uncomfortable.

"Hello, Liza."

She ignored him, and turned her attention to Eloise. "I didn't know you were invited," she said.

Eloise pursed her lips, clearly offended. "Of course I'm invited. Why wouldn't I be? This gala was my idea. There's certainly no money in the city budget for something like this, so I'm practically footing the bill for this whole affair."

Liza wanted to laugh in her face, and she bet the only reason Eloise funded the party was so she could continue to find favor with Anthony. "Let's go freshen up," Eloise said, before turning to Anthony. "Why don't you go and check on the guests."

A rowdy, boisterous voice was heard in the corridor where Liza had emerged a few moments earlier.

She cupped her ear. "I think I hear our friend Jack now."

Liza caught Anthony's eyes, and she thought she saw

his head shake back and forth slowly, but couldn't be sure in the low light of the room.

Eloise touched Liza's elbow. "Follow me, before we have to listen to one of Jack's corny jokes."

They walked in the opposite direction, down another low-ceilinged corridor until they came to the powder room.

Liza didn't have to use the facilities. She only wanted to get Eloise away from Anthony, but while she was there, she figured she might as well check her makeup.

She opened up her small purse and brought out a nude lipstick. As she was applying it, she got the sense Eloise was waiting for her to finish before she started to talk.

Sure enough, as soon as Liza had replaced the cap, Eloise spoke.

"That's a lovely dress," she said.

"Thank you," Liza replied. "Yours is, too."

This was a flat-out lie. Eloise's gown, which appeared to be yellow silk, was embroidered with white butterflies. Liza thought it was the ugliest thing ever.

"Yellow is my happy color," Eloise said, peering at her reflection in the mirror. "But black hides everything."

She slanted her eyes toward Liza, and in the mirror, she could see Eloise staring at her scar.

"Well, almost everything," Eloise finished, with a hint of a sneer.

Liza felt her cheeks get hot at the cutting remark. What did this woman have against her? Was it her relationship with Anthony? Or something else?

She lifted her chin, ignoring the urge to touch her scar.

It doesn't matter, she told herself. Despite her jealousy, she knew she had to ignore her feelings and play nice with Eloise. The woman was a key investor in the clinic, and it wouldn't do to make her angry. She had to keep the peace.

More importantly, Liza knew she had to keep believing Anthony cared about her.

She masked a smile, as the memories of her and Anthony, and what they had done together, flashed back into her mind.

If the passion he'd displayed for her previously was any indication, she didn't have to worry that Eloise Bradshaw and her manufactured breasts and filler-enhanced face would steal his heart.

Anthony Marbet was hers, and hers alone. He couldn't stay away forever, and neither could she. Liza knew she loved him and it was about time she admitted her feelings to him, even if he didn't love her.

"Would you excuse me?" Liza asked, and she left before Eloise could respond.

She returned to the courtyard and discovered that more guests had arrived, so she followed the throng to the outside patio, where everyone else had gathered. She looked over the crowd, trying to spot him, or at least a familiar face, and saw none.

There was a jazz band in a far corner near the home, while opposite them, under a bright red-and-white striped awning, were tables lined with platters of hot and cold hors d'oeuvres.

Liza felt her stomach burble with hunger, but she

knew she couldn't eat a thing until she'd had a chance to speak to Anthony.

She was on her way to the open bar set up beneath three huge palm trees, when she felt a tap on her shoulder.

She turned and saw Vanessa, holding a champagne flute filled with orange juice. She wore a black-and-gold minidress that tastefully accentuated her baby bump.

"Enjoying the gala?"

Liza smiled. "I just got here, and was just on my way to get a glass of wine."

Vanessa saluted her with her glass. "Have one for me?" She reached back and pressed her hand against her back. "I can't wait until this child is born. I feel like I'm about to burst."

Liza didn't know whether to laugh or agree. Vanessa did look much larger than she did the last time Liza saw her, but she was one of those women whose beauty was enhanced by pregnancy. She simply glowed.

"Good thing Anthony is here," Liza remarked. "Although I'm not sure if he knows how to deliver a baby."

Vanessa gave her a conspiratorial grin. "All doctors know how to deliver a baby. They just don't want you to know it."

Liza laughed and looked around. "Where are the future grandma and grandpa?"

She was referring to Gregory's mother and father, the owners of the estate. She wanted to meet them and inquire about the architect who built their home. As a small business owner, it was necessary to network, whenever and wherever she could.

"My in-laws are in Hawaii, so they aren't here."

Liza gasped. "I've always wanted to visit there."

The two women strolled to the edge of the patio. The Langston home sat on a high cliff, overlooking the Pacific Ocean. The sun was beginning to set, painting the blue sky with slashes of pink and orange.

"I know. Me, too. I guess we'll both have to be satisfied with this fabulous view," Vanessa giggled. "I think I fell in love with the view first, and my husband second."

"I barely know you, but you and the mayor seem insanely happy," Liza confided. "What's your secret?"

Vanessa thought a moment. "He accepts me for who I am, and I accept him. Faults and all."

"It sounds like hard work," Liza commented. "Or an impossible dream. Or both."

"With the right person, it's neither. It's just love."

Liza stared out at the horizon, where it seemed like the ocean just stopped. But beyond her vision, the Pacific went on for thousands of miles, until its waves crashed upon the shore of another land.

Just love.

If it were only that simple.

With my mother and my father.

With Anthony and me.

"There you are. I've been looking all over for you."

She recognized Mayor Langston's voice and turned around to see him embracing Vanessa.

"I don't know how you could have missed us," Vanessa laughed, rounding her hands over her baby bump.

He gave her a kiss so tender that Liza blushed, and

she almost turned around to give the couple their privacy. Instead, she cleared her throat.

Vanessa and Gregory separated, but he kept his arm draped over her shoulder.

"Liza, it's great to see you again."

She nodded her greeting. "I'm happy to be here."

"I certainly hope so. You're the woman of the hour!"

Liza raised a brow. "What do you mean?"

A waiter suddenly appeared and Gregory placed Vanessa's now-empty flute on his tray.

"Dr. Marbet has your renderings of the clinic displayed inside, and everyone is raving about the design and it's not even built yet."

The warm glow of acceptance curled inside her. "It's not often that people appreciate the aesthetics of a building so soon, or at all."

"Sounds like you're not going to have any problems establishing yourself in Bay Point," Vanessa said.

"I'd also like you to consider being on our building and land committee," Gregory added. "We need someone like you to ensure that the historical integrity of Bay Point is maintained throughout the town's redevelopment process."

Vanessa shushed him. "This is no time to talk about work, honey. You promised me a dance."

"I promised you two dances," he replied, kissing her on the cheek. "Liza, will you excuse us?"

She nodded and waved goodbye as Gregory whisked his wife away to the dance floor. The band was playing an old R & B tune, not too fast and not too slow. She tapped her foot in time with the beat, as she watched the couples bump and sway, ignoring the urge to go look for Anthony.

Liza pursed her lips. As far as she was concerned, he should be looking for her.

She decided to continue on to the open bar, to get the glass of wine she'd been wanting all along, when she spotted a familiar face mulling over the choices at the hors d'oeuvre table.

"Doc Z! I didn't know you would be here!"

She gave him a hug. He was thinner than she remembered, but his embrace was just as strong.

"I told Anthony that if he didn't invite me, I'd reverse the A plus I gave him back at Harvard."

Doctor Zander's raucous laugh lifted a few heads around them, most of them older females.

Liza smiled. "How are you doing?"

A smile crinkled the edges of his deeply tanned face. "I'm hanging in there as much as these old bones will let me." He shrugged. "You never know. The night is still young. I may run away with one of these beautiful ladies yet."

"If Mama was alive, she would have been first in line," Liza said, her smile fading. "And who could blame her for wanting to chase after you? My father never paid her any attention."

Liza had tried to keep her voice light, but could still hear an edge of bitterness in it.

She loved her father, and though he was kind, by his actions, he'd driven a wedge in the family. He had chosen other women over his wife. Lots of them.

Doc Z led her away to a corner of the patio. It was

getting darker now and the tiny white lights strung along the low hedges lent a festive glow. But right now, she felt anything but happy.

"Your mother had a lot of issues."

Liza crossed her arms. "Yes, and my father was one of them."

"I know…and I know it hurt your mother deeply," Doc Z admitted.

She stared at him, and then sank against the cream-colored stucco of the house. She'd always suspected Doc Z knew about her father's infidelities. The two men had been the best of friends. But to have it confirmed was a blow.

Liza dropped her chin, eyes burning with tears.

She focused on her toes, the nails painted bright red, not wanting to believe what she was hearing, but knowing it was true. Doc Z had no reason to lie to her. It was time she admitted the truth, at least to herself.

"Despite his faults, he loved her," he continued. "Perhaps too much.

Her head shot up. "And yet, he cheated on her, even though he knew how fragile she was about her looks?"

He nodded, and she shook her head in disbelief.

"Maybe if he hadn't cheated on her, she wouldn't have felt she needed all those fillers. All those surgeries," she said. "She wouldn't have died trying to keep looking young."

Doc Z shrugged and leaned against a white column. "We all knew she was beautiful. She was a former model. But she didn't. She just never believed it herself—on or off the runway."

Liza looked away and was rubbing at her jaw with the ridge of her knuckles, something she did out of habit when she was upset, when Doc Z reached over and brought her hand in front of her face.

"Don't fall into the same trap as your mother did," he warned.

Liza feared it was too late. Instead of focusing on her inner beauty, she'd concentrated on her physical flaws, often to the detriment of her own happiness and relationships with men.

Anthony had told her he thought she was beautiful, but had she unconsciously driven him away by thinking she wasn't?

She inhaled a deep breath. "In some ways, I think she sabotaged herself. Unlike me, she wasn't a strong person. Once her modeling career was over, she had nothing but her looks to fall back on."

"Count your blessings. You're young. You're intelligent. And you're gorgeous."

Liza grinned. "And you were always so wise."

"Yeah? Better grab on to my advice now, before it disappears into my softening mind."

She laughed and gave him a grateful hug.

"Just because you were my favorite teacher in med school, doesn't give you the right to steal my woman."

Liza stepped back, as Anthony approached them. Her heart swelled in her chest at his words.

My woman.

"Oh, pardon my intrusion, kind sir," Doc Z said, in a mock British accent. "I thought she was just your architect."

"And I thought I saw a scotch with your name on it at the bar," Anthony shot back.

Though his roughened tone was good-natured, there was no doubt in Liza's mind that Anthony meant business.

Doc Z raised a brow. "I can take a hint as well as I can tie a suture. But if I were you, I wouldn't let this woman out of your sight."

Anthony adjusted his black bow tie, his gaze piercing hers.

"I don't plan on it." He took her hand in his. "Come on, Liza. I've been waiting to speak with you all night."

Anthony took Liza by the hand and led her down a sandy path. There was an enclosed gazebo at the far edge of the Langston estate, which would give him the privacy he needed.

"Where are we going?" she asked.

"Just trust me, okay?" he answered, in an irritable tone.

As they made their way down the path, the music got softer and softer, sounding a bit mournful in his ears.

Since his self-imposed "break" from Liza, he'd missed her terribly. Though his concentration was better, his mood had taken a turn for the worse.

"Can you slow down," Liza demanded, putting her hands on her hips. "I'm getting sand in my stilettos."

Anthony stopped and huffed out a breath. "How come every time I see you, you're wearing inappropriate shoes?"

Liza tilted her head, as if she were trying to think of

the shoes in her wardrobe. "What do you mean, every time?"

"Forget it. I'm carrying you the rest of the way."

He picked her up and she pummeled her hands on his back. "Put me down, Anthony!"

But a smile crossed her face and he refused.

Minutes later, they reached the white-clapboard gazebo. He was sweating from rushing, and from nerves, and he loosened his bow tie.

Anthony had every intention of just talking to her, but when he looked at her beautiful body in his arms, his desire for her could no longer be ignored.

He set her down gently on a fabric-covered bench and when he opened his mouth to speak, she grabbed onto his neck and drew him to her lips in a passionate kiss.

It wasn't long before he was sitting alongside her, licking her neck, and drawing down the straps of her bra with his fingers.

He lifted her dress, not bothering to take it off, and removed the thong from her rear.

"I've missed you, Liza."

The only sounds that mattered were her moans, as she straddled and moved and clung, driving them both into a wild frenzy, while the waves spilled onto the shore far below.

After they had come, he had laid her gently back on the bench. Kneeling before her, with slow and deliberate licks of his tongue, he made her climax once more.

She'd grabbed his head, gritted her teeth and held

on, and he felt the pleasure he'd invoked reverberating through her entire body.

Liza tasted so good that he wanted to continue, but she was moaning so loud, he was afraid they'd be discovered.

Liza gasped, sat up and smoothed down her dress. "What do you think you're doing, Anthony? We're supposed to be at the gala."

He slipped back into his pants and zipped up. "I think we're having a lot more fun right here, don't you agree?"

"Yes, but I don't understand," she said, running her fingers through her hair. "I thought you wanted a break from me, from us."

He put his shirt on, but left it unbuttoned. "I was wrong, Liza. Over these past several months, I've had a lot of time to think."

"Me, too." Her lips trembled. "What are you saying, Anthony?"

He knelt before her and took her hand in his, squeezing it tightly. "I'm saying that I love you, Liza, and I don't want to lose you. Not ever."

"But what about your work at the hospital, and the clinic? You said I was distracting you, and a relationship with me would only make it worse."

Anthony looked deeper into her eyes, praying he could make her understand. "I know. But I realized that being apart from you was a mistake. I was just scared you would leave me. Not many women can deal with my hectic schedule and lofty ambitions."

Liza gave him what appeared to be a tentative smile.

"I would never leave you, Anthony. I told you, I'm your partner. We have a written contract, remember?"

"Yes, of course, but let's put business aside, okay?" He took a deep breath. "I feel that we could work better together as a couple than as two individuals trying to deny our feelings for each other."

He cradled her face gently between his palms, and gave her a gentle kiss.

"You do love me, too? Don't you, Liza?"

He watched her eyes well with tears. "Yes, I love you, Anthony. So much that it hurts."

"I know I can cure your pain, all of it, past, present and future, if you'll let me," he told her, brushing the wetness from her cheeks with his fingers.

Her eyes sparkled. "But what about our other agreement? To not mix business with pleasure?"

He mimed ripping up an imaginary piece of paper. "Consider it null and void."

"I think we've broken it several times already," Liza said, laughing.

"I'd like to talk about another contract," he broached. Her face registered confusion and he was barely able to hide his excitement. "The contract of a lifetime together."

He reached into his pocket and took a deep breath before presenting her with a large diamond ring.

He watched her eyes widen as he slipped it onto her finger. "Liza, will you marry me?"

She nodded in agreement, curling her arms around his neck, pressing her lush body against his.

"Now, why don't we celebrate?"

Liza slipped his shirt from his shoulders and he kissed her with more love and passion than he thought either of them could bear, knowing that their journey together was just beginning.

Epilogue

"I'm going to miss this place...and you!"

Liza ran her hand over the antique mahogany bureau in her third-floor room at the bed-and-breakfast, tears brimming in her eyes. Despite the room being very small and filled with old-fashioned furnishings, she'd grown accustomed to the space. In a way, it had become her sanctuary.

Maisie swiped her finger along the edge, checking for dust, and not finding any, grunted with satisfaction.

"Aww...honey. I'm not going anywhere and neither are you! Bay Point is your home now. You and Anthony are part of the family."

The two women embraced, and Liza gently pulled away for fear of suffocating in Maisie's overpowering perfume.

"I can't wait to see that grand new house you've built."

In the midst of overseeing the construction of the clinic, she'd also designed and built her first home, where she and Anthony would live and love each other.

With a sly grin, she tucked a few last-minute items into her suitcase.

But Maisie wasn't having it. Nothing got past her.

"What's that smile for?"

"Oh, I'm just thinking how much fun it will be to have you and Prentice over for dinner, just as soon as Anthony and I get back from our honeymoon."

Maisie rubbed her palms together. "Ooh. A double date! Maybe the old man will spring for a corsage from Vanessa's flower shop!"

Maisie arranged Liza's veil over her bare shoulders and down her back as carefully as she would cut out her famous biscuits.

Though Maisie had become a dear friend, for a moment, Liza wondered what it would have been like if her mother would have been helping her get ready.

She would have tried to hide her scar, first with her choice of wedding dress, high necked, then choice of veil, probably with enough tulle to make a scarf. Despite everything, Liza knew she would have welcomed her mother's intrusion on the most important day of her life.

How many times does a woman get married? she thought and picked up the small arrangement of roses, daisies and baby's breath. She held it in front of her waist, like she'd practiced so many times earlier in the week.

"If the corsage is as beautiful as this bouquet," she giggled, "you should ask him to marry you!"

Maisie finished fixing the veil and put her hands on her hips. "No way. One wedding in a lifetime is plenty for me."

Liza hugged her again, not caring if her veil was askew.

"Thank you for everything, Maisie. For allowing Anthony and I to get married here."

Maisie shooed her away. "If you thank me one more time, I'll play the lottery," she warned. "And I don't even believe in gambling."

She stepped over to the window and drew the lace curtain aside. Liza joined her and they both looked down into the backyard, where the wedding party and guests were gathered.

Mayor Langston, who was Anthony's best man, was there, along with Vanessa, holding their one-year old daughter.

Trent, who had jokingly agreed to be the ring bearer though none was needed, was sitting alone, looking gorgeous and vaguely uncomfortable at the same time.

Doc Z was back in town for a visit. He was surrounded by a gaggle of Bay Point's most eligible older women vying for his attention. Liza pinpointed the one to whom she would toss her bouquet.

She let the curtain fall and turned to Maisie. "The last eighteen months sure have been a roller-coaster ride."

The clinic had opened the week prior without a hitch. Anthony already had a six-month waiting list for new patients before he even opened the doors.

"That's the fun part of life," Maisie replied. "Not knowing where the next curve is coming."

"Or where it's going to take you."

She stepped to the corner of the room and stared into the full-length mirror for a long moment, admiring what she saw reflecting back at her.

Her strapless ivory wedding gown was a perfect fit, and she knew Anthony was going to love it.

So much had changed for Liza in the past year, most of all, her opinions about herself. It had been a struggle, but she was finally starting to shed her mother's opinions of beauty and establishing her own: ones that focused on building herself up, instead of tearing herself down.

"You are a beautiful bride."

"I am, aren't I?" Liza replied in a clear, strong voice.

"Ready for the day you'll never forget?"

Her lips trembled, and her heart felt like it was going to leap out of her chest. "I'm nervous, Maisie. What if—"

"Hush now. You deserve to be happy, Liza," she said fiercely, shaking her finger. "Don't let anyone or any situation in life take that away from you."

Liza nodded and the two women looped arms. Between managing her gown and Maisie's bad knees, the trip down three flights of stairs was slow.

However, it seemed only moments later that she was outside in the California sunshine, walking down the redbrick aisle, and standing in front of the minister saying "I do" to the most wonderful man she'd ever met.

Her Anthony.

* * * * *

REQUEST YOUR FREE BOOKS!

2 FREE NOVELS
PLUS 2 FREE GIFTS!

KIMANI™
ROMANCE

Love's ultimate destination!

YES! Please send me 2 FREE Harlequin® Kimani™ Romance novels and my 2 FREE gifts (gifts are worth about $10). After receiving them, if I don't wish to receive any more books, I can return the shipping statement marked "cancel." If I don't cancel, I will receive 4 brand-new novels every month and be billed just $5.44 per book in the U.S. or $5.99 per book in Canada. That's a savings of at least 16% off the cover price. It's quite a bargain! Shipping and handling is just 50¢ per book in the U.S. and 75¢ per book in Canada.* I understand that accepting the 2 free books and gifts places me under no obligation to buy anything. I can always return a shipment and cancel at any time. Even if I never buy another book, the two free books and gifts are mine to keep forever.

168/368 XDN GH4P

Name	(PLEASE PRINT)	
Address		Apt. #
City	State/Prov.	Zip/Postal Code

Signature (if under 18, a parent or guardian must sign)

Mail to the **Reader Service:**
IN U.S.A.: P.O. Box 1867, Buffalo, NY 14240-1867
IN CANADA: P.O. Box 609, Fort Erie, Ontario L2A 5X3

Want to try two free books from another line?
Call 1-800-873-8635 or visit www.ReaderService.com.

* Terms and prices subject to change without notice. Prices do not include applicable taxes. Sales tax applicable in N.Y. Canadian residents will be charged applicable taxes. Offer not valid in Quebec. This offer is limited to one order per household. Not valid for current subscribers to Harlequin® Kimani™ Romance books. All orders subject to credit approval. Credit or debit balances in a customer's account(s) may be offset by any other outstanding balance owed by or to the customer. Please allow 4 to 6 weeks for delivery. Offer available while quantities last.

Your Privacy—The Reader Service is committed to protecting your privacy. Our Privacy Policy is available online at www.ReaderService.com or upon request from the Reader Service.

We make a portion of our mailing list available to reputable third parties that offer products we believe may interest you. If you prefer that we not exchange your name with third parties, or if you wish to clarify or modify your communication preferences, please visit us at www.ReaderService.com/consumerschoice or write to us at Reader Service Preference Service, P.O. Box 9062, Buffalo, NY 14240-9062. Include your complete name and address.

KROM15

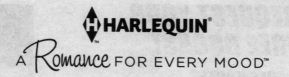

HARLEQUIN®

A *Romance* FOR EVERY MOOD™

JUST CAN'T GET ENOUGH?

Join our social communities
and talk to us online.

You will have access to the latest
news on upcoming titles and special
promotions, but most importantly,
you can talk to other fans about your
favorite Harlequin reads.

Harlequin.com/Community

Facebook.com/HarlequinBooks

Twitter.com/HarlequinBooks

Pinterest.com/HarlequinBooks

"You're all cloak and dagger." Nate nodded at the way
she held the menu in front of her face. "Unless you need
glasses.

The way she frowned was cute. The corners of her
mouth turned down and her bottom lip poked out. A
shoe made direct contact with his shin. "My eyesight is
perfect."

"Not just your eyesight." Nate cocked his head to get a
glimpse of the hourglass curve of her shape.

"Does your cheesy machismo usually work on women?"

Nate flashed a grin. "It worked on you last week." He regretted the words the second before he finished the *K* in week. Amelia's foot came into contact with his shin again. "Sorry. Chalk this up to being nervous."

Amelia settled back against the black leather booth. "You're supposed to be nervous?"

"Who wouldn't be?" Nate relaxed in his seat. "You breeze into town and drop a wad of cash on me just to make me do work for what you could have hired someone else to do, and much more cheaply, too."

The little flower in the center of her white spaghetti-strap top rose up and down. Even through the flicker of the flame bouncing off the deep maroon glass candleholder, he caught the way her cheeks turned pink.

"Let's say I don't trust anyone around town to do the work for me."

Don't miss HIS SOUTHERN SWEETHEART
by Carolyn Hector, available October 2016
wherever Harlequin® Kimani Romance™
books and ebooks are sold!